D1071548

366 Graces

About the Compiler

John Allport served in the Metropolitan Police Service for 30 years, retiring in 1991. For most of his service he was a Detective Sergeant combatting major crime in Central London. During his career he was stabbed twice and shot at on three separate occasions by criminals . Following the last shooting in both legs with a sawn-off shotgun, John took two years to learn to walk normally again.

He has been elected Man of the Year, and received the National Leaders Award for work in aid of the disadvantaged in London. He has won a Prince of Wales Committee Award, and has received four medals from Her Majesty the Queen, including the British Empire Medal and the Queen's Gallantry Medal.

Drawing by Mary Steward of Southwold

366 Graces

plus 24 for fun

Comprising the very best of the old
favourites, with an original collection
of many new graces written especially
for this book.

Compiled by
John Allport

Edited by Emily Hewitt

Highland Books

GODALMING
SURREY

First published in 1998 by Highland
Books Limited, 2 High Pines, Knoll
Road, Godalming, Surrey, GU7 2EP
(www.highlandbks.com) Reprinted
2002

Cartoons "MAC" of the Daily Mail

The jacket includes image number
492062 from the Corel Professional
Photo collection, which is protected by
copyright. Used under license.

I S B N 1-897913-41-9

Printed in South Africa by CTP Limited.

Foreword by Betty Boothroyd, former Speaker of the House of Commons

One of the earliest words that any child utters is "ta" and as they grow up we teach them the importance of "saying thank you".

Human beings are understandably distressed if we do not show any appreciation of kindness, consideration and generosity. Not to show gratitude is rightly seen as churlish and rude.

Of course, God does not need to be thanked. He gives generously and seemingly indiscriminately; as equally to the ungrateful as to those who are appreciative of his gifts. But that does not remove from us the obligation to recognise His bounty, to "say grace".

This book contains a magnificent and wide-ranging compilation of graces. It shows us how we can say "thank you" to God in so many different ways and styles for what we receive from His ever open hand.

I have no doubt this book will be widely used and appreciated.

Contents

This book has been specially designed to be carried in the pocket, so that you can take it with you to a function, where you have been, or may be called upon, to say grace.

Introduction

There can hardly be a child of my generation who at some time or other has not uttered the immortal words *'For what we are about to receive may the Lord make us truly thankful'*. They conjure up images of overcooked cabbage, boiled potatoes and rhubarb and custard.

In post-war Britain we were duly thankful for school dinners before which grace was always said. Later, when I entered college, grace was said before every meal and on feast days sung with great gusto. Certain pious families would even sing grace while standing around the table in the hotel dining room!

The custom has now gone from many schools but it continues to be followed at public functions and formal occasions and is being resurrected by many families throughout the country.

As it is believed that graces have been said for at least 2000 years and probably longer, many different forms have developed. The essence of any grace is to give thanks to God for his provision but, as this book demonstrates the authors of graces have considerably expanded their brief over the years. The shortest grace in this collection has in fact no words and appropriately enough is a Quaker grace where everyone joins hands and bows their head for a silent moment.

The shortest audible grace sticks to the original formula—"eucharisteo" *I give thanks*. It's probably safe to assume that God is the one being thanked. The Royal Navy, never known to waste words assume nothing and with admirable brevity intone—*Thank God... Amen.* Admiral Lord Nelson, while respecting brevity pushed the boundaries further back with—*God Save the King. Bless our dinners. Make us thankful. Amen.*

Frequently, the one invited to say grace at a formal gathering is not the one who is asked to deliver the main speech, thus it is not surprising that some have used the grace to deliver a mini-address. Alcuin of York (735—804) gave a bold lead when he virtually preached a sermon (Page 34) and his example has been followed by many including the author of this introduction.

The dear old Victorians show the way when it comes to expesssing their flair for instructing the young in what they believed to be moral values. *The Table Rules for Little Folk (Page 93)* would either increase the appetite because of its length or deaden it because of its content. One verse from the six recorded in this book is enough for now:

> I must not scold or whine or pout
> nor move my chair or plate about.
> With knife or fork or napkin ring
> I must not play, nor must I sing.

More poignantly, a grace found in a book which tells of country life in Suffolk in the 1850's speaks of the grim humour of the poor.

> Heavenly father, Keep us alive,
> There's ten of us for dinner,
> And grub for only five.

Over the years graces have been written for what is now called 'specialist interest groups'. Rugby clubs 'Munching their lunch;' Cricketers 'with no overs left tonight,' and a reminder that cricket is the only game where meals are written into the rules.

As children have often been required to say grace there are many humorous examples. My particular favourite is:

> There was once a goose and a wren,
> who gave lunch for a cock and a hen,
> 'O Lord' prayed the goose,
> 'Bless these gifts to our use
> And ourselves in thy service ... Amen'

Those called upon to say grace at formal events sometimes fall back on humour. Not everyone can get away with a humorous grace but Desmond Tutu certainly can because his own faith is permeated with humour and sincerity. His grace on page 61 is surely a classic.

A grace when the food doesn't look too attractive

*(but don't let it be known why
you have chosen this one)*

We thank you Father for this food
which is so much better
than any one of us deserves ... Amen.

This book of 366 graces for all occasions will certainly become an essential volume for toastmasters and their ilk, together with ordained and lay ministers who can almost guarantee they will be called upon to say grace at any function they attend. However, in addition it is my hope that this book will find its way into many homes throughout the world and that it will encourage families to resurrect an ancient custom of thanking God for his care and goodness.

'All this is for your benefit, so that the grace that is reaching more and more people may cause thanksgiving to overflow to the glory of God' *2 Corinthians 4:5.*

Terry Waite

Some Thoughts on Graces

Grace is a word with a hundred meanings. It may mean almost anything, or nothing much, or something both attractive and important. Is it a Christian name or a surname, for singers, princesses or cricketers? Does it describe style or movement, from athletes to eagles? Or something religious, like that remembered acronym, *G*od's *R*iches *A*t *C*hrist's *E*xpense?

It may be a prayer; runner up to the best known and most used from the Bible, and a handy way to bring a meeting or a service to an end. Or could it refer to that old custom of grace before or after meals?

This sort of grace may sound like some hangover from boarding school, ancient clubs or colleges, or the Victorian dinner table. Not a bit of it.

One great value of this book is in rescuing the concept of "saying grace" from what it *seems*—a party piece to recite—to what it can be at its best—a humbling word of sheer and sincere gratitude. An acknowledgement that we didn't make this food and drink ourselves; a reminder that while we eat, some others cannot; a pointer to the Creator and Redeemer whom some at least want to remember before raising knife and fork to the main business.

Suppose some at the table do not share the presuppositions of the prayer? They can switch off for a moment in deference to their host's quaint custom, or they can keep listening, and learn something. Or the host may suggest a silent observance, or at least introduce something less demanding than the Apostles' Creed.

With characteristic charm and whimsy, Charles Lamb raised the whole matter back in 1823. He wondered why we didn't say grace before music, or going for a walk; presumably he knew the obvious answer. Short graces, he said could seem irreverent; long ones, impertinent. "We sit too long at our meals" he wrote, "to be able with any grace to say grace". And graces are embarrassing and dissonant "at the heaped up boards of the pampered and luxurious".

Nearly two hundred years ago he anticipated a reaction against his novel doctrines. "I hear somebody exclaim—Would you have Christians sit down at table, like hogs to their troughs, without remembering the Giver?—no—I would have them sit down as Christians, remembering the Giver, and less like hogs". True "Graces" are much more than a form of words.

But in our own day, do people actually eat meals at all? More and more of us eat out, they tell us; grace may not be easy to the sound of music, or the noisy banter from the next table. Those who still eat at home may be simply grabbing a yoghurt from the fridge, or more likely groping blindly at the pizza on their lap, eyes glued to the flickering coloured box in the corner.

There is actually no situation where "Grace" is impossible! Picnics up the mountain, snacks on the train, formal receptions, coffee in a smoke-filled transport cafe ... and why ever not? How dare we sit down to feed our faces without so much as a nod (hopefully, rather more) to the One who provides it all for his world? If devout Jews and Muslims don't hide their faith away in shame, why on earth should I?

Last year we were in Tanzania. That is a country in the bottom twentieth of the world's economies on anyone's scale; in some lists, it's the bottom one. Not to mention refugees spilling over its borders in recent years, and aid-vultures zooming in to sponge on other people's tragedies; but that's another story—I think.

Come with us on a ten-hour drive over bumpy tracks to a village in the middle of nowhere. Our son Tim calls at the door "Hodi, Hodi!" (response, "Karibu!—Welcome!") and introduces us to his friends in the dark little shed that is their home. We are invited in (of course!) and after the initial wondering greetings, out to the back goes our hostess, followed by wide-eyed toddlers—to return with, what? A tray holding three bottles of 'soda'—Mirinda fizzy orange.

That could happen in England? Keep watching. The lady asks Tim if he would ask me, Baba Tim, to say grace. She doesn't mind which language; I settle for English. The occasion demands something more than "For what we are about to receive ..."; I hope Charles Lamb would not have minded. And that story was repeated in many homes in towns and villages across that needy, welcoming land.

Now drop into McDonalds—and spot the difference. Who are the cultured, civilised people—let alone the Christian nation?

But this is fast becoming a sermon—something a "grace" should never do. So I may as well go the whole hog, if I may risk that expression here.

Jesus said grace. He said it in his own way, on the hillside, at home, or at special meals with his friends. By precept he shows us how to ask for our bread, and by example, to give thanks for it. Are we so mature that we know better than the Son of God?

I will grant to Charles Lamb one more word. "Graces" he says "are the sweet preluding strains to the banquets of angels and children"—yes, and adult mortals too. John Allport's labour of love, and faith, can help us to be a little more childlike, a little more angelic, and a great deal more human.

Christopher Idle

Graces at Breakfast

*Grace for an early breakfast,
or a meal at a dawn vigil*

Lord, another day is dawning,
And another meal is spread;
So we bow our heads and humbly,
Thank you for our Daily Bread. Amen.

*A breakfast grace for a
wonderful new day*

Father, we thank you for the night,
And for the pleasant morning light;
For rest and food and loving care,
And all that makes the day so fair. Amen

For fellowship of faith and love

Give us this day our daily bread,
O Father in heaven,
and grant that we who gather here
in the fellowship of faith and love,
may take our food with gladness
and simplicity of heart.
from The Abbey of New Clairvaux collection

A grace for a cooked breakfast

Praise God, we did not have to forage,
for eggs or bacon, toast or porridge*;
and thank God too for our enriching,
by all those working in the kitchen.
Amen.

Christopher Idle

*or, marmalade, milk, flakes etc;
but porridge must stay

*A breakfast grace asking God to remain
with us through the day*

We thank you, Lord, for this good food.
Be with us as we eat it,
And stay with each one of us
throughout the coming day,
In your name we ask it. Amen.

*A farmhouse grace
at breakfast time*

For sweet milk and pure water,
For crisp cereals and brown eggs,
For fresh bread and creamy butter,
We thank you, dear Father. Amen.

Graces at Breakfast

The Kellogg grace for
breakfast time

Dear Lord, keep us from being like por-
ridge,
Stiff and stodgy and hard to stir.
Rather make us like cornflakes,
Fresh and crisp and ready to serve.
Amen

Attributed to Bishop Colin Docker
often used by Lawrence Jackson

Graces at breakfast, lunch, tea and supper

Christians pray 'Give us this day our
daily bread' and they remember to
thank God for it. They also remember
that 'man cannot live by bread alone'
but on the word of God, the Bread of
Life. Let us thank God for *that* food and
this and ask that we may use both for
the good of our souls and bodies.

Michael Saward

A grace before a simple breakfast

Morning is here
The table is spread,
Thanks be to God
Who gives us our bread. Amen.

*A grace seeking dependability
in following the Lord*

Dear Lord,
As we follow you today,
May we be like porridge
solid and dependable
and like cornflakes …
quick and ready to serve. Amen
Robert & Sharon Buxton

A short breakfast grace

For bacon, eggs and buttered toast,
thank Father, Son and Holy Ghost.
Amen
John Peake

The Quaker porridge oats grace
(just so cornflakes don't get all the praise!)

O Lord,
keep us from being like cornflakes,
Hard and brittle and easy to crumble,
Rather make us like porridge,
warm and soft and full of goodness.

from Robin King

A grace at a mid-day meal
Thank you Father, for this meal
At the centre of our day;
Give us grace
To keep you in the centre of our lives.

Leslie Stradling

A grace for a luncheon
The grace He gave that we might be
forgiven.
The grace we need that leads us up to
heaven.
For grace to love and to appreciate;
For grace to dwell awhile before we eat,
Now grace; to offer thanks to Him who
gave us most,
Before we tuck into our *vegetables and
roast! Amen

John Allport

* or for breakfast — our marmalade and toast.

*A grace to God who grants blessings
to all his creatures*

At breakfast, dinner-time and tea,
Our grateful thanks we raise to Thee,
Who sees the meanest sparrow fall,
And grants His blessing to us all. Amen.

A mealtime grace for wholesome food

Gratefully we bow our heads,
And pause again to say.
Thank you for the wholesome food,
Which you supply each day. Amen.

A grace asking His help to enjoy our food

Thank you very much, Lord,
for this food and drink.
Help us to enjoy it,
neither gorging it
nor wasting it.
For Jesus sake. Amen.

Michael Saward

A grace that we may be ready to serve

Lord, give us those qualities
Which describe our *Hors d' oeuvre* -
Make us tasteful, top of the list,
And ready to serve. Amen

Leigh Spicer

A grace at the main meal of the day

For bread, vegetables, meat and sweets
{mention whatever is on the table}
And for the hundreds of good things you
give us,
We thank you Lord. Amen

Leslie Stradling

A Grace for all the family at teatime

Let's hold hands and give God thanks
for Jesus' sake,
Let's dwell; before our sandwiches and
cake.
Let's thank him at this and every other
meal.
Let's all enjoy our children's happy zeal.
Let's rejoice in friendships, love and
laughter.
Let's go on serving God, today,
tomorrow and thereafter. Amen

John Allport

A grace for God's presence at our table

Father in heaven,
Be present with us now
as we gather together,
that we may eat and drink
to the glory of your Name.
Grant this through Christ our Lord.

from Margaret Straub

Suggested grace before the evening meal

Bless us, Lord God,
and all these gifts
which we gratefully receive
from your loving hand:
through Jesus Christ our Lord. Amen

from Caldey Abbey

A supper-time grace

For sleep to refresh us,
For family to love us,
For food to satisfy our hunger,
We thank you, Lord. Amen

A grace at an evening meal

The night has come, the board is spread,
Be with us Lord, and bless our bread.
Amen.

Leslie Stradling

Graces after meals

A responsive grace after meals

Bless the Lord, O my soul,
And all that is within me, bless his holy name.
Bless the Lord, O my soul,
and forget not all his benefits.
Blessed be God, eternal king,
for these and all his good gifts to us.
Amen.

Celebrating Common Prayer
The Pocket Version printed 1994 p. 274
based on Psalm 103 vs 1—2

Grace after meals

Almighty God, we thank you for the
food which you have given us. May we
always use your gifts to give you glory
and so be worthy to be called your
children:
through Jesus Christ our Lord. Amen

from Caldey Abbey

Grace after meals

Eternal Father, bless us as we rise from
the table
and grant us your grace.
Grant to our family, our friends and all
who follow us,
the alms of mercy as the eternal food of
the soul
and to all who are here, and are to
come, a share in paradise.
Through Christ our Lord. Amen

*This grace was frequently used by the old
people of Ireland as a prayer after communion. I cannot trace its origin. Contributed
by John Baptist Hasbruck from the
Guadalupe Abbey Collection, Lafayette,
Oregon, U.S.A. and probably sent to his
Abbey in America from the Abbey of Mount
Melleray in Ireland*

Responsive grace after meals

All your works praise you, O God,
And your faithful servants bless you.
They make known the glory of your
kingdom
And speak of your power.
For these and all God's gifts and graces,
let us bless the Lord.
Thanks be to God. Amen

Celebrating Common Prayer
The Pocket Version printed 1994 p.274

Grace after meals

We give you thanks, Father,
for these and all your blessings.
Increase our gratitude
and deepen our desire to share with all
the good things we receive from you.

from Margaret Straub

Grace after meals
Mile buiochas — 'a thousand thanks'.

A thousand thanks to you, Lord God,
for your goodness in giving us this food;
may it give life to our souls.
Grant food to those who are in want.
If today we show improvement,
may we, our family and our friends,
be better sevenfold one year from today.
Through Christ our Lord. Amen

*This grace was collected in the Arran Isle off
the West Coast of Scotland in the Firth of
Clyde by Diarmuid O Laoghaire. Sent by John
Baptist Hasbruck from the Guadalupe Abbey
Collection, Lafayette, Oregon, U.S.A.*

Grace after meals

Lord, you have filled us with good
things.
Hear our thankful prayer
and open your generous hands
to the starving poor of the world.

from Margaret Straub

Grace after meals

Eternal glorious Father of heaven,
You have given us this food;
grant us also the alms of mercy
and the glory of eternity to our souls,
and to every soul who seeks it.
Through Christ our Lord. Amen.

*This grace originates from Uibh Ratach in
Kerry. Sent by John Baptist Hasbruck from
the Guadalupe Abbey Collection, Lafayette,
Oregon, U.S.A.*

Grace after meals

O God, source of all goodness,
we thank you for the food that was laid
before us,
and for your loving-kindness to us
and to all your children.
Forgive the evil we have done
and the good we have left undone,
and raise us up to newness of life
in Jesus Christ our Lord. Amen

from Caldey Abbey

A grace after sharing together

For these gifts,
For those with whom we
have shared them
For the freedom to enjoy both,
We bless you Father, through Him
Who is your greatest gift of all—
Jesus Christ our Lord. Amen

Mother Sheila

Grace after meals

Almighty God,
We thank you for the food we have
enjoyed,
which you have given us.
Feed us with your grace
and deliver our souls from the death of
sin
through Jesus Christ our Lord. Amen

from Caldey Abbey

*A grace by a young person reflecting when
getting ready for bed*

Dear Jesus,
When I undress for bed,
I like to say a little prayer
Each night upon my knees,
for mummies who prepare
our breakfast, lunch and teas.

Grace after meals

Father in heaven,
Your will was the food and drink
of him you sent.
Grant that we may also accomplish your
work,
in the likeness of Jesus Christ your Son.

from Margaret Straub

Grace after meals

We thank thee Lord for this our food,
Much more because of Jesu's blood.
Let manna to our souls be given,
The Bread of Life sent down from
Heaven.

from Mrs M. Cambridge

Grace after meals

Father, Lord of heaven and earth,
grant us thankful hearts
and a spirit of eagerness
to share with our brothers and sisters
all that you have given us.
through Christ our Lord.

from Margaret Straub

Grace after meals

Almighty God, by whose hand we live
and move and have our being, we
thank you for the food which you have
given us. Guard us in body and soul and
keep us from all evil:
through Jesus Christ our Lord. Amen

Caldey Abbey

Grace after meals.

Father, we thank you for all your blessings.
May our gratitude intensify the prayer we offer for all who are in want.

from Margaret Straub

Graces remembering the providers.

A grace bestowed

Heavenly Father,
We accept gratefully the gifts
You have bestowed on us through...
[naming the cook]

Oberammergau

A grace for health and fellowship

For food and all who prepare it,
For health and fellowship and all who share it,
And mindful always of all who need it,
We thank thee, Lord our God. Amen

Collected by Ruth Clarke

A little girl's grace

God bless this food to my tummy,
God bless the person who cooked
it—mummy,
God bless daddy who is sometimes
home late,
But who earns the money to put food on
our plate
God bless James my brother, and my
granny too
And God, please take care of yourself
—Because if anything happens to you …
We've had it. Amen

A grace for good food

For all who sow and harvest,
for all who prepare and serve
good food upon our table;
Accept our thanks O Lord. Amen

John Allport

Grace from Scotland,
remembering the providers

No ordinary meal—a sacrament awaits
us
On our table spread,
For men are risking lives on sea and
land,
That we may dwell in safety and be fed.

A grace remembering the provider(s).

Heavenly Father,
We are constantly amazed at the variety
of food which you have provided for our
wellbeing.
As we anticipate the enjoyment of the
meal before us now, we thank you for
the many who have had a part in its
provision:
the growers and harvesters, the
transporters and shopkeepers and
especially a big thank you for the one
(those) who has (have) prepared it all
for our table today.
In Jesus' name. Amen

Bridget Langley

Some Medieval Graces

A sermonet on Christ's grace

Lord Christ, we pray thy mercy on our
table spread,
And what thy gentle hands have given
thy men
Let it by thee be blessed: what'er we
have
Came from thy lavish heart and gentle
hand,
And all that's good is thine, for thou art
good.
And ye that eat, give thanks for it to
Christ,
And let the words ye utter be only peace,
For Christ loved peace: it was himself
that said,
'Peace I give unto you, my peace I leave
with you.'
Grant that our own may be a generous
hand
Breaking the bread for all poor men,
sharing the food.
Christ shall receive the bread thou
gavest his poor, and shall not tarry to
give thee reward.

Alcuin of York 735—804

An early 10th-century bishop's grace

Hunger and thirst, O Christ, for sight of
thee,
Came between me and all the feasts of
earth.
Give thou thyself the Bread, thyself the
Wine,
Thou, sole provision for the unknown
way,
Long hunger wasted the world wanderer,
With sight of thee may he be satisfied.

Radbod, Bishop of Utrecht c.900AD

Elizabethan Graces

Elizabethan Grace

Pray we to God, the Almighty Lord,
That sends food to beasts and men,
To send this blessing on his board,
To feed us now and ever—Amen.

Book of Private Prayer—1553

A 16th- century grace inviting Jesus to be
present at our table

Come, Lord Jesus, be our Guest
May this food to us be bless'd. Amen.
  Attributed to Martin Luther 1483—1546
A favouite grace of George Carey. He says that
when his children were growing up the Carey
family used this Lutheran grace.

A grace compiled for Elizabeth 1

God bless our food: God guard our ways
God give us grace, His Name to praise.
And ever keep in ways serene,
Elizabeth our gracious Queen.
      A traditional grace used by Noel Jones

For food and drink we praise You

O God, your presence is so Fatherly,
Now for food and drink; we praise you,
Because everything that nourishes and
strengthens us is given by your hand.
Amen

              A 16th-century Grace printed on
              a serviette in a Swiss Hotel

A grace asking God for just a little 'extra'

God! to my little meal and oil
Add but a bit of flesh, to boil:
And thou my pipkinnet* shall see
Give a wave-offering unto thee.

Robert Herrick 1591—1674
* A small earthenware vessel

*An Elizabethan grace to remind us
of all Christ means to us*

And when thou art at thy meat praise thy
God:
in thought at ilke* morsel and say thus
in thy heart:
Loved be thou King
and thanked be thou King
and blessed be thou King.
Iesu all my joying
of all thy giftes good
that for me spilt thy blood
and died on the rood.
Thou give me grace to sing
the song of thy loving
my praise to thee ay spring
withouten any feigning.

from the Lay Folk's Mass Book
* at that—or each

A 16th-century grace

To God who gives our daily bread
A thankful song we raise,
And pray that he who sends us food
May fill our hearts with praise.

Thomas Tallis 1505—1585

A 16th-century Royal grace

The eyes of all things do look up
and trust in thee;
O Lord, thou givest them
their meat in due season.
Thou dost open thy hand and fillest
with thy blessing everything living.
Good Lord, bless us and all thy goods,
which we receive of thy bountiful
liberality;
Through Jesus Christ our Lord. Amen.

Queen Elizabeth 1 1533—1603
suggested by Psalm 145

An Elizabethan cook's grace

For bread and salt, for grapes and malt,
For flesh and fish and every dish:
Mutton and beefe and all meats cheefe:
For cow-heels, chitterlings, tripes and
sowse,
And other meate that's in the house:
For backs, for breasts, for legges, for
loines,
For pies with raisons, and with proines:
For fritters, pancakes and for freyes,
For venison pastries, and minc't pies:
Sheephead and garlick, brawne and
mustard,
Wafers, spic'd cakes, tart and custard,
For capons, rabets, pigges and geese,
For apples, carawaies and cheese:
For all these and many moe,
Benedicamus Domino.

God give us grace

God bless our meal,
God guide our ways
God give us grace
Our Lord to please
Lord, long preserve in peace and health
Our gracious Queen, Elizabeth.

G. Bellin 1565
from Michael Mann

*A grace written by a Devon farmer in the
reign of Queen Elizabeth 1*

Now we have both meat and drink
Our bodies to sustain,
Let us remember helpless folk
Whom need doth cause to pain.
And like our God is bountiful
For giving us much store,
So let us now be merciful
In helping of the Poor.
Then shall we find it true indeed
God will forsake us never,
But help us most when we have need
To whom be praise for ever.

sent by Eric Evans

Some 16th, 17th and 18th Century Graces

*May we always have the grace
to say thank you*

Thou that has given so much to me,
Give one thing more—a grateful heart;
Not thankful when it pleases me,
As if thy blessings had spare days;
But such a heart, whose very pulse
may be thy praise.

George Herbert 1593—1633
A favourite grace of
Walter Hargreaves-Wragg

A 17th-century grace

You who give food to all flesh,
Who feeds the young ravens that cry
unto you
And has nourished us from our youth
up,
Fill our hearts with goodness and
gladness
And establish our hearts with your grace.

Lancelot Andrewes 1555—1626
sent by Keith Jones

A grace by John Milton

Let us with a gladsome mind,
Praise the Lord for he is kind.
All things living he doth feed
His full hands supply their need. Amen

John Milton 1608—1664
A favourite grace of John Low

17th-century grace for all
meals great and small

What God gives us, and what we take,
'tis a gift for Christ his sake;
Be the meal of beans and peas,
God be thanked for those, and these.
Have we flesh, or have we fish,
All are fragments from His dish.
He his Church save, and the king,
And our peace here, like a spring,
Make it ever flourishing.

Robert Herrick 1591—1674

An 18th -century grace

Be present at our table Lord,
Be here and everywhere adored:
Thy creatures bless, and grant that we
May feast in paradise with thee.

John Cennick 1718—1755
The favourite grace of John
Mockford and John Durrant

An 18th -century grace thanking
God for his providence

Almighty King, whose wondrous hand,
Supports the weight of sea and land,
Whose grace is such a boundless store,
No heart shall break that sighs for more.
Thy providence supplies my food,
And 'tis thy blessing makes it good;
My soul is nourished by thy Word,
Let soul and body praise the Lord.

William Cowper 1731—1800

Graces for our daily needs

A grace for our daily needs and
good health to enjoy them

For food and friendship,
For wine and wisdom,
For music and merriment,
And for good health to enjoy them all,
We give you thanks, O God,
in Christ's Name. Amen

Michael Saward

A grace for a humble grateful heart

Dear Lord,
When we feel too proud, too angry
and too clever,
When we are so selfish and satisfied,
Give us a humble heart,
Make us grateful for all your gifts,
Especially that for us, Jesus died. Amen

David Porter

A grace asking for God's mercy

O God, protector of those who trust you,
without you nothing is strong, nothing
is holy.
Bless this food which we eat in your
honour,
and increase your mercy towards us:
through Jesus Christ our Lord. Amen

from Caldey Abbey

A grace thanking God for his invitation

Father, you are the host
And we are your guests:
Thank you for inviting us
To sit at your table. Amen.

Leslie Stradling

Personal Graces

A personal grace to share with others

Loving Father,
For food when we are hungry,
for drink when we are thirsty
for friendship when we are lonely
for fuel when we are cold, and
for compassion when we are in need.
We give you thanks in Christ's name.
Amen

Michael Saward

*A grace for refreshment of
both body and mind*

For this refreshment of body and mind,
Let us be thankful to Thee,
Giver of all good things. Amen

collected by Haydn Maddock

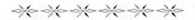

Grace for caring for each other

Father,
Bless our sharing of these gifts,
our living of this day,
our care of each other,
to their good and your Glory.
Through Jesus Christ our Lord.

Mother Sheila

Part of a refectory grace
from Chester Cathedral

Give me a good digestion, Lord,
And also something to digest;
But when and how that something
comes
I leave to thee, who knowest best.
Amen.

Collected by Robin G. Laird

A personal grace

Bless me, O Lord,
And let my food strengthen me to serve
thee,
For Jesus Christ's sake.

Isaac Watts 1674—1748

A grace to share in God's heavenly banquet

Giver of all gifts,
Burden our hearts with your promise,
Let our lives prefigure the heavenly
banquet
when all nations of earth will be
gathered
into a garden of peace.

John B. Giuliani

A grace of personal dedication

Bless, O Lord, this food to my use,
and myself to your service,
through Jesus Christ our Lord . Amen

A grace for a more interesting menu

Heavenly Father, you provided John the
Baptist
with locusts and wild honey:
Thank you for providing us with a more
interesting menu.

by Leslie Stradling
A favourite grace of Desmond Tutu

A grace of thanks that all things are good

May God be praised
That All things are so good
For those who love him. Amen

John Donne

A grace for our daily bread,
the gracious gift of God

If we have earned the right to eat this
bread,
Happy indeed are we:
But if unearned, still you give it us,
May we more faithful be. Amen

A Musicians' grace

Lord, let our pancakes be flat,
our sauces sharp,
our flavouring natural;
our scales correct and not canned,
our fingering exact and not hasty:
Let all our parts be in time
and our organs in tune;
may our meal develop in pure harmony,
moderato, vivace, sostenuto;
and make our keynote—generosity,
our chorus—gratitude,
and our programme—filled with
appreciation
Of all today's arrangers,
and of our original Creator and
Composer. Amen.

Christopher Idle

The Miller's grace—remembering
God is the provider

Back of the bread is the flour,
Back of the flour the mill,
Back of the mill is the wind and the
shower,
And the sun and the Father's will.
For mill and flour, and sun and shower,
We thank you now O Lord. Amen

Miss E.J. Allen-Williams found at Felin Crewi
Water Mill, Penegoes, Machynlleth

A Fisherman's grace

Let us give thanks for this array
where none of it can get away.
We did not have to catch it all;
Lord, help us to dispatch it all;
For here we are not cold or wet
we need no boots or bait or net,
one fellowship of line and rod
enriched by all the gifts of God! Amen

Christopher Idle

A Good Friday grace
with fishermen in mind.

We thank you, Lord. for these your gifts,
And ask your blessing for those who
with unfailing courage,
and faithfulness risk their lives daily to
bring them to us. Amen

Graces from Scotland, Ireland and Wales

The Revd Sandy Millar, Vicar of Holy Trinity Church, Brompton say he finds Robert Burns an excellent source for graces. Here are just four of his better-known, with a sense of humour.

The Selkirk grace

Some ha'e meat, and canna eat,
And some would eat that want it;
But we ha'e meat, and we can eat,
And sae the Lord be thankit.

A grace to God of nature wide

O Thou who kindly dost provide
For every creatures want.
We bless thee God of nature wide
For all thy goodness lent.
And, if it please Thee, Heavenly Guide,
May never worse be sent.
But whether granted or denied,
Lord bless us with content.

Grace before meat

O Lord, when hunger pinches sore, ·
Do thou stand us in stead,
And send us from thy bountious store
A tup—or wether-head *

* Mutton.

An after-dinner grace remembering
those waiting on the table

O Lord, since we have feasted thus,
Which we do so little merit
Let *Meg** now take away the flesh,
And *Jack* bring in the spirit.

                Robert Burns 1759—1796

* Meg the serving girl—and Jack the
potman in the tavern

A traditional Irish grace

May the food God provides us here be
blessed.
And when we have enjoyed our meal
and part,
May the road rise to meet you,
May the wind always be at your back,
May the sun shine warm on your face,
The rain fall softly on your fields,
And until we meet again
May God hold you in the palm of his
hand.
Amen
Being Irish, a favourite grace of Robin G. Laird

A truly Welsh grace

Bendithia'n bwyd, ein nefol Dad,
Y rhai mewn eisiau clyw eu llef,
A rho i'n henaid fara'r nef.
Bless our food, O Heavenly Father,
And make our society a pleasure.
Hear the cry of those in need,
And give our soul the bread of heaven.
Amen

A Welsh grace of hope and love

Risen Lord,
We thank you for love, laughter, bread,
wine and dreams.
Fill us with green growing hope,
And make us people whose name is
love. Amen

Adapted from words found
by a Welsh craftsman

*A grace from Caldey Island,
off Tenby, Dyfed, Wales*

God of all power, and source of all good,
bless this food which we eat
in honour of your name.
Implant the love of you in our hearts,
and strengthen us in your service:
through Jesus Christ our Lord. Amen

from Caldey Abbey

Favourite Short Graces

Grace over the meal

This is Yours,
We are Yours
Bless them as they meet.

Martin Shaw

A short celebration grace

For this celebration, for all those
gathered here
and for this meal, we thank you Lord.
Amen

John Allport

A short grace which says it all

For every cup and plateful
Lord make us truly grateful. Amen

Revd A.S.T. Fisher M.A.
Chaplain of Bryanston School,
Dorset—1930

The favourite grace of James Bailey aged 7 of
Halesworth and James Hewitt aged 7 of Loudwater—who likes to get on with his meal!

A grace from the church office

Whenever we eat
may we remember God's love.

St Peter's Church, Loudwater

A grace for all His gifts

For all Your gifts and our daily food,
We bow our heads in thanks O God.
Amen

John Allport

A grace for good fellowship and friends

For food and for fellowship,
For friendship and for families
Thank God. Amen

used by Martin Partridge on 7th September
1996 at the wedding of his daughter Drusilla to
Jonathan Harris

A short grace and to the point

Thank you Jesus for our food. Amen.

The favourite Grace of brothers
Peter (5) and James (3) Halliwell

God bless our food

May the food God provides us here be
blessed. Amen

Gordon Wilson of Enniskillen
November 1990

A grace to share in His feast

Blessed be He who calls us to His feast
For He is God, for ever and ever. Amen

Lord, fill us with what is good!

Lord, when our bodies and souls are empty,
fill us with what is good,
for Jesus sake.

Keith Jones

A short grace thanking God for all his gifts

Thank God for all.

Garth Norman

A well known short grace

Bless this food to our use
And us to thy service. Amen
A favourite short grace of
John Low

A short Latin grace

Benedictus Benedicat.
(May the Blessed One give a blessing)
A favourite grace of Charles Taylor

God's holy name be praised

For these and all His holy mercies,
God's holy name be blessed and praised.
Amen.

said by James Atwell
St Edmund's Friends Day Luncheon 20.7.96

Graces for fun

God has a sense of humour and above
all he is forgiving, and these *graces for
fun* are included in addition to the 366
graces.

Mark Twain in Huckleberry Finn had
something to say about graces:
'When you got to the table you couldn't
go right to eating, but you had to wait
for the widow to tuck down her head
and grumble a little over the victuals,
though there warn't really anything the
matter with them.'

"A" Out of the mouths of youngsters
comes forth the truth!

My father was a Vicar and we always said
grace before every meal, and as we children
got older we were encouraged to make our
contribution by saying an extempore grace.

The vicarage was a hub of activity in the
1950s with many comings and goings. At
one teatime when I was seven I was asked to
say grace. I was very embarrassed by the

visitors present, so my father tried to help and be encouraging by saying, "say what your mother said this morning."

After hesitation and very sheepishly I enquired if my father really wanted me to repeat what my mother said that morning. He replied. "Oh yes dear boy. Go on you have nothing to be afraid of." So with great reverence I prayed:

"Oh dear we have those awful people coming to tea today. Amen!"

If nothing else this is probably an unusual grace.

Mark Hutchinson

"B" After dinner grace—'Pass the brandy'

The Regimental Padre was unexpectedly
absent from a special mess dinner and a
young Oxbridge educated officer who
had enjoyed a good repast and was full
of wine was asked to say grace after the
meal. He cast about in his mind and
produced:

> 'Benedictine Benedecantur'
>
> Ronald Smythe

*"C" A grudging thanks after a school
meal!*

We thank the Lord for what we've had,
If it had been more, we should have
been glad,
But as the times are rather bad,
We thank the Lord for what we've had.
> —then a very loud Amen is given
>
> Miss A.H. Chadwick

"D" A weight watchers grace?

Thank you, God,
for breakfast, lunch and dinner
If it weren't for you
I'd be much thinner. Amen.
J. Stubbs

*"E" A Royalist's grace during the time of
Oliver Cromwell often pronounced
'CRUMWELL'*

God, send this crum well down!

Author unknown
dated 8th April 1642

"F" A grace for a powerful constitution

A friend of John Bilyard (see "L" below)
who was a missionary in Africa for most
of her working life and from a climate
where the quality of food was
unpredictable, she recalls applying the
frequently used sailors grace
but in more modest terms:
Lord, if I get it down,
Will you please keep it down Amen.

Joy Grindey
Missionary in Africa

*"G" A grace for some respite
from long speeches*

Lord, who blessed the bread and wine,
We ask your blessing as we dine;
And if long speeches we endure
Pray God, they serve a good liqueur

Robin G Laird

"H" A grace for a good appetite

O Lord, make us able,
To eat all on this table. Amen

Mervyn, Lord Horder

"I" For a Rugby Club luncheon

Lord, to say thanks to you first's the crunch,
Now please, bless this hungry bunch,
Before they munch their lunch.

Adapted

"J" A grace when the food doesn't look attractive

[but don't let it be known why you have chosen this one]
We thank you, Father, for this food
Which is so much better
Than any one of us deserves. Amen

by Leslie Stradling

A favourite grace of Archbishop Desmond Tutu

"K" Bless the Lord

The Revd Hargreaves-Wragg tells the story of a bishop who attended a civic banquet, and who was asked to say grace AFTER the meal. He rose ponderously to his feet, and uttered these words:-
"Bless the Lord O my soul;
and for all that is within me,
bless His holy name!"

"L" A grace—not to be recommended!

John Bilyard writes,
My own memory of school grace is
somewhat jaundiced. As a new boy I
was persuaded to join some older boys
in a protest against the quality of the
school dinners. The protest involved
're-writing' the last line of the traditional
grace so we would say:

"For what we are about to receive
May the cooks be shot."

Of course, when it came to it,
Bilyard—wanting to be one of the
lads—was the *only one* to say it that
way. I literally *carried the can* for that,
being made to put the leftovers (which
were copious) into the pig bins for
weeks.

*"M" A rebel schoolgirl's parody of a
standard grace*

For what we have left on our plates,
May the school chickens be truly
grateful.

Miss A. H. Chadwick

*The situation regarding school meals
appears to be universal—even at a
girl's school!*

"N" A Victorian children's grace

God bless this food,
And make us good
For Jesus sake. Amen
    written by an ever-hopeful grown up!

"O" A grace for another miracle

O Lord who blessed the loaves and fishes
Please look down upon these dishes,
And though the salad be but small,
Lord make it plenty for us all.
But if our stomachs it does fill,
t'will be another miracle.
    collected by Angela Radmal

"P" Many a slip 'twixt cup and lip!

The well known theologian, Professor
Denis Nineham told Bishop Noel Jones
of the Isle of Man of a slip he made once
when saying grace.

  "God, bless these gifts to our use
  And keep us needful of the minds of
  others".

When the slip-up in the second line was
pointed out to him, Denis Nineham
replied after a pause,"I'm more
intelligent than I thought".

"Q" *The well-travelled evangelist Arthur Blessit,*

(his life story can be read in 'Arthur—a pilgrim')
in his travels across the world would always pray the same way before he ate. As he was often confronted with dishes which would certainly require an effective prayer, he would simply pray: "Lord, kill it! Whatever is in it, Kill it!" Not very eloquent, but doubtless effective!

Matt Frost

"R" *Army dinner on board a Naval ship off the Falkland Islands in the early 1980s*

Sailing round in this old tin tub,
we're living on a boat.
We thank thee Lord for the galley and the grub,
And for keeping us afloat.

Roy McAllen

"S" *A Nursery Limerick*

There was once a goose and a wren,
who gave lunch to a cock and a hen,
"O Lord," prayed the goose,
"Bless these gifts to our use
And ourselves in thy service." Amen.

A favourite of Terry Waite

Graces for fun

"T" A grace for no regrets!

For food and wine we give you thanks,
dear God our Father;
But may we also on the morrow,
regret not too much of either. Amen.

Peter M Rutherford

*"U" The Navy get the gravy,
but the Army get the beans!*

For boiled and roast,
For beans on toast,
Thank Father, Son and Holy Ghost.

Michael Mann

"V" grace when eating out
*A favourite grace of those who don't like
washing up.*

For well filled plate
and brimming cup
and freedom from the washing up!
We thank You, Lord. Amen.

"W" Grace for a meal where some of the expected guests have not yet turned up.

Lord, thank you for good health, good cheer,
and every mouthful on our plate;
be present with us gathered here,
and bless our friends who maybe late;
God speed them on their journey through
lest we should have to eat theirs too.
Amen.

Christopher Idle

'...Lest we should have to eat theirs too.'

Graces for fun

"X" A British Army Boxer's Grace
Lieutenant General The Honourable Sir William Rous KCB OBE wrote in July 1996:

'I heard a charming Grace a few weeks ago, but it needs to be put in context. I am President of the British Army Boxing Association and was invited to attend The Army Boxing Team's Annual Dinner arranged to celebrate an outstanding season. The boxers, all junior ranks in their late teens and early twenties, made all the arrangements themselves, and decided on a formal occasion in a Sergeants' Mess at Aldershot. It fell to the youngest boxer present, Private Charlton, to say the Grace and this is what he said:
"Thank God for good food and good wine; and please, God
—help all the boxers get up in the morning. Amen."'

Private Charlton
The British Army Boxing Team—1996

Graces from Abroad

When boiling water for tea

I pray thee Lord,
To send down spiritual fire,
To burn away the coldness of my heart,
That I may always be hot-hearted in serving thee.

Prayer of a Chinese Christian woman.

A Nicaraguan grace

O God, bless this food we are about to receive,
Give bread to those who hunger;
and a hunger for justice to us who have
bread. Amen.

A Hebrew grace

Blessed are you, Lord God of all creation.
You hold in your care all that you have
made.
Bless us as we share this meal,
and touch our hearts to serve all whom
we meet;
through Christ our Lord. Amen

> Based on the Hebrew blessing,
> 'Berakhah Attah Adonai'

A German grace

Bless the food upon the dishes,
as you blessed the loaves and fishes,
As the sugar's hid in the tea,
So may our lives be hid in thee. Amen

Grace from Sri Lanka

As the water falls on dry tea leaves
and brings out the flavour, so
may the Holy Spirit fall on us,
So that we can bring refreshment to
others.

(Source—C.M.S. Newsletter)

Jesus said grace—He took the five loaves and gave thanks to God.

Jesus took the five loaves and the two fish,
Looked up to heaven, and gave thanks to God.
O Lord who fed the multitudes with five barley loaves,
Bless what we are about to eat.

Arabic Grace from Egypt.

A grace of love and joy from America

Lord Jesus, be our holy guest,
our morning joy and evening rest,
and with our daily bread impart,
your love and peace to every heart.
Amen.
Heard, remembered and memorised by a monk from Guadalupe Abbey, Oregon while staying at a nearby Trappist Monastery

A short Greek grace.

"eucharisteo."
[I give thanks.]

used by Anna Sorensen.

A grace of friendship from America

God of grace,
Sustain our bodies with this food,
Our hearts with true friendship,
And our souls with your truth.
For Christ's sake Amen.

A grace from Wrentham, Boston,
Massachusetts U.S.A.

May God bless our meal
and grant us a compassionate
and understanding heart
towards one another. Amen

from Margaret Straub

Prayer of a hungry man in South Africa

God of our fathers, I lie down without
food,
I lie down hungry,
Although others have eaten and lie
down full.
Even if it be but a polecat, or a little rock
rabbit,
Give me and I shall be grateful!
I cry to God, Father of my ancestors.

Baralong, South Africa.

A grace from South Africa for every good gift

Giver of every good gift,
Bless us your people in our receiving,
Our giving and our sharing. Amen.

Leslie Stradling

A grace from Latin America

Bendice Senor nuestro pan
y da pan a losque tienen hombre
y hombre de justicia a los que tienen pan;
bendice Senor nuestro pan.
translated: Bless, Lord, our bread
and give bread to those who are hungry
and hunger for justice to those who have
bread; bless, Lord, our bread.
A grace sung in San Carlos de Bariloche, brought
back from Argentina and
translated by Mr Marcus & Mrs Clare Idle

A grace from Puerto Rico—West Indies sharing both dependence on God and generosity

God, give us enough for our family to eat
today and for everyone who comes to
our door.

from Ken and Sarah Corson

Christopher Idle who sent this grace said Ken & Sarah Corson are former Methodist Missionaries in South America, founders of the Southern Institute for Appropriate Technology (SIFAT) in Alabama, also known as: Servants in Faith and Technology.

United Nations Grace

Grace at the 1995 Annual Dinner of the United Nations Association, Isle of Man

The Government is now upon His
shoulders,
The Saviour Jesus Christ our Lord;
We look for peace in attitude
That binds us as a cord.
And thus, we sit and eat this food
prepared;
Our guest is Jesus Christ the Lord;
We bow our heads in gratitude
You're in our hearts adored.

Robin Oake

Graces for all occasions

Grant us, Father

Father, grant us the generosity
to be truly thankful for these gifts now
before us.
Grant us the humility
to receive that which others have prepared.
Grant us the compassion
to remember the needs of those who
hunger.
Grant us the strength
to do justice, to establish peace and to
walk
in your ways. Amen.

David Sheppard

A grace for food from many countries

Heavenly Father,
For food from many countries,
for food of all the seasons,
for those that harvest and
for the service of many hands—
we give you thanks.

John Allport

A grace thanking God for his
abundance, after the meal

We give you thanks, O Lord,
for your abundance from which we have
received,
for the love you have placed in our
hearts,
O Saviour of the world, who live and
reign for ever and ever. Amen

from The Abbey of New Clairvaux collection
Vina, California, U.S.A

A grace reflecting our dependence on God

Bless O Lord, before we dine,
Each dish of food, each glass of wine,
And make us evermore aware
How much O Lord we are in your care.
Amen.

Collected by Robert Firth.

Grace after meals—thanking God for his
love and asking for forgiveness

O God, source of all goodness,
we thank you for the food that was laid
before us,
and for your loving-kindness to us
and to all your children.
Forgive the evil we have done
and the good we have left undone,
and raise us up to newness of life
in Jesus Christ our Lord. Amen

from Caldey Abbey

*Grace at a gathering of neighbours for a
meal or a large gathering for
a common purpose*

May God be praised who taught us all,
That we should be good neighbours,
And offer proof beyond fine words,
Resulting from our labours.
And so we give our thanks to Him,
For one Man's good example.
And ask His blessing on this meal,
We are just about to sample.

Lawrence Jackson
said at the 1992 Person of the Year Luncheon
Hilton Hotel, London

*A grace remembering to eat our food
in honour of God*

Almighty God,
You sent your Son to eat even with
sinners,
Bless this food which we eat in honour
of your name, and sanctify us by your
presence:
through the same Jesus Christ our Lord.
Amen

from Caldey Abbey

Bless our food and drink

Bless us, O Lord, bless our food and drink;
you have purchased us at great price,
free us from evil.
Through Christ our Lord. Amen

from the Guadalupe Abbey Collection
Lafayette, Oregon, U.S.A.

For the richness of God's grace

Father, through your bounty we receive,
All the needs by which we live,
For the richness of your grace
Now receive our grateful praise. Amen

John Allport

A grace asking God for an inner understanding in the breaking of bread

Bless our hearts,
to hear in the breaking of the bread,
the song of the universe.

John B. Giuliani

A grace for God's strength

O God, source of all goodness,
your strength is made known in our
weakness.
Bless this food, and strengthen us in
your service:
through Jesus Christ our Lord. Amen.

from Caldey Abbey

Give us grace to do Your will

Bless, O Lord, this food which we are
about to eat for our bodily welfare.
May we be strengthened thereby
to do your holy will.
Through Jesus Christ our Lord. Amen

from the Guadalupe Abbey Collection

A grace for friends to share our meal

For food to eat and those who prepare it,
For health to enjoy it and friends to share it
We thank you Heavenly Father.

Henry Lunney

A grace asking God for a cheerful spirit

Almighty God, as we gather to eat,
give us:-
grateful hearts,
truthful lips,
merciful pockets,
careful digestions,
cheerful spirits,
and fruitful lives,
through Jesus Christ our Lord. Amen
                                    Michael Saward

A grace for Spiritual food

Bless this food, O Lord,
to the use of our bodies;
feed us with the Bread of Life,
for Christ's sake. Amen
                            W. Hargreaves-Wragg

Glory, praise and thanks to God

Glory, praise and thanks to you, O God,
for this food and our good health.
We also thank you for all the food and
health
for which we have not thanked you.
Through Christ our Lord. Amen
                    from the Guadalupe Abbey Collection
                            Lafayette, Oregon, U.S.A.

A grace that we may with thanks receive

Lord of all, thy creatures see,
Waiting for their food on thee,
That we may with thanks receive
Give, herewith, thy blessing give;
Fill our mouths with food and praise;
Taste we in the gift the grace,
Take it as through Jesus given,
Eat on earth the bread of heaven. Amen.

Charles Wesley.

A grace praising God for all that is good

For life and love and rest and food,
For daily help and nightly care,
Sing to the Lord for he is good,
And praise his name for it is fair.

John Samuel Bewley Monsell 1811—1875 tune:
'Gonfalon Royal' by
Percy Carter Buck 1871—1947
Oxford University Press

A grace seeking God's promised reward

Almighty and most merciful Father,
bless this food which we eat in honour
of your name,
and grant that, free from sin,
we may swiftly reach the happiness of
your promises:
through Jesus Christ our Lord. Amen

from Caldey Abbey

A 'Verve Cliquot' lunch celebration
[which can be adapted in line 3
to any sponsor of a charity luncheon]
Today our treat of wine and meat
will feed our thoughts of food.
Bless those who serve our fare with
Verve
to keep us in good mood.
Remember God prepared the soil,
supplied the rain and sun;
And those the fare did help prepare
We thank them, everyone. Amen

Roger Young

The Johnny Appleseed grace

The Lord is good to me,
and so I thank the Lord
for giving me the things I need
—the sun, the rain, the apple-seed:
The Lord is good to me!
And every seed I sow
will grow into a tree
and someday there'll be apples fair
For everyone in the world to share,
The Lord is good to me.

This is a favourite in America and when asked
for one of his favourite graces, Noel Tredin-
nick responded by singing it! 'Johnny Apple-
seed' was an American preacher who used to
go around planting apple seeds as well as the
seeds of the bible

A grace extending our trust in God

For these and all Thy mercies given,
We bless and praise Thy name, O Lord.
May we receive them with thankgiving,
Ever trusting in Thy Word.
To thee, alone, be honour, glory,
Now and henceforth for evermore. Amen
                              chosen by Robert Firth.

*A grace thanking the Giver of all good
things*

We bless the Giver of these
[the food before us spread]
and all good things,
through Christ our Lord. Amen
Tim Butlin

A Responsive Grace before meals

The eyes of all wait upon you, O God,
*And you give them their food in due
season.*
You open wide your hand
*And fill all things living with
plenteousness.*
Bless, O Lord, these gifts to our use
and us to your service;
relieve the needs of those in want
and give us thankful hearts;
for Christ's sake. Amen.
Celebrating Common Prayer,
The Pocket Version printed 1994 p.274

Graces for all occasions

A grace not to live by bread alone

Blessed are you O Lord,
who have the words of life!
Grant that we may not live by bread
alone,
but by every word that comes forth
from the mouth of God.
This we ask through Christ our Lord.
Amen

from The Abbey of New Clairvaux collection

Grace asking for all God's blessings

Lord, bless our ears with your word.
Bless our bodies with your bounties.
Bless our lives with your love.

from Margaret Straub

A grace for a gracious heart

O God and father of us all,
We thank you for this food and wine,
And in our plenty—graciously incline,
Our hearts and our thoughts,
In kindness and mercy,
To those not nearly so well provided.
Amen.

Collected by Robert Firth.

A grace to God of day and night

O give thanks to Him who made,
Morning light and evening shade,
Source and giver of all good,
Nightly sleep, and daily food.
Quickener of our wearied powers,
Guard of our unconscious hours. Amen
Josiah Conder 1836.

*A grace for us all to gather in God's
kingdom.*

As the bread that was scattered upon
the mountainside
was gathered together to fill twelve
baskets,
so may all the people of God
be gathered together into one kingdom.
Attributed to Fr. Hillary Greenwood
A favourite grace of Simon Pettitt.

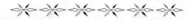

*A grace for spiritual blessing through
God's revealing Word*

Father,
Bless this food which re-creates
our bodies.
May the hearing of your word
re-create our souls.

from Margaret Straub

Grace to the Giver of all good things

Father, you are the giver of all good
things,
Give us also grateful hearts
for all your love to us, through
Christ our Lord.

Keith Jones

A grace for an appetite to eat

God, who givest mouths for meat,
And today has blessed our board,
Give us appetite to eat
To the glory of the Lord. Amen.

A.S.T. Fisher
a favourite grace of John Murrell

A grace thanking God for his goodness

Bless these thy gifts, most gracious God,
From whom all goodness springs;
Make clean our hearts, and feed our
souls
With good and joyful things. Amen

A grace of gratitude

Accept we ask, O Lord,
Our humble and hearty thanks
for the gifts of food and wine set before
us—
deepen our gratitude,
enlarge our sympathies
and order our affections,
in generous and unselfish lives. Amen

Collected by Robert Firth

*A grace by a man to whom God and his
family meant everything*

For family and friends,
For fellowship and food
Father, we thank you. Amen

Stanley Sallows 1901—1979,
thatcher and Lay Elder

*A grace thanking God for all He
shares with us*

Almighty God,
You have given us a share in the divinity
of him who shared our humanity.
We thank you for the food you have
also shared.
Bless it now as we eat it in honour of
your name, and fulfil your work in us:
through Jesus Christ our Lord. Amen

from Caldey Abbey

Graces for all occasions

A grace to remember Jesus at meal times

Thy glory here we make our aim,
To eat and drink in Jesu's name,
Nor live to eat, but eat to live,
Our food we now with thanks receive
Amen

Charles Wesley

A grace by the Poet Laureate

For these and all His other mercies,
above all the crowning mercy
of serious conversation,
God's name be praised.

Alfred Austin 1835—1913.
Poet Laureate from 1896

An International Police Grace

Grace used at the 1996 European Association of Airport and Seaport Police Conference at Gibraltar. (The first line can be adapted)

For Conference and fellowship
of the E.A.A.S.P.,
Accept our thanks, Lord, for this food,
Which we eat gratefully.
Keep us within your care, O Lord,
And may this be our goal:
In serving others true and right
With body, mind and soul.

Robin Oake

Grace at a Barristers and Counsel Dinner

A grace for God's Truth

We thank you, Heavenly Father,
For good food and brotherly love,
Relief for all in need we pray,
Your Truth—our aid from day to day.

collected by Haydn Maddock

Grays Inn: Before dinner:

Bless, O Lord, us and these gifts,
Which by thy goodness we are about to
eat.

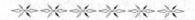

Grays Inn: After dinner:

Accept for thyself, Almighty God,
Thanks for thy gifts,
through Jesus Christ, Our Lord. Amen

Edmund Davies

Graces for Children and Schools

Quaker grace

- Joining hands -
Everyone at the table joins hands ,
close their eyes and bow their heads for
a silent moment.

The Cadbury Family
Bourneville, Birmingham

Father, bless us all our days

For food and all Thy gifts of love,
We give Thee thanks and praise.
Look down, O Father from above
And bless us all our days.

A grace thanking God for all things good

God, we thank you for this food,
For rest and home and all things good;
For wind and rain and sun above,
But most of all for those we love.

Maryleona Frost

Thanking God for being together

We thank you Lord, for happy hearts,
For rain and sunny weather,
We thank you Lord, for this our food,
And that we are together.

Emilie F Johnson

A grace from a very young child

Dear Jesus,
Thank you for our food. Amen

Lucy Partridge, age 3

A grace for Children

Great God and Father,
for all that you give us;
family
friendship
food, and
fun,
we give you thanks.
Help us
to enjoy them, and
to serve you.
In Christ's name. Amen

Michael Saward

A grace for something different

Lord God, you fed the children of Israel
With manna and quails:
Thank you for feeding us your children
With a better diet than that.Amen.

Leslie Stradling
A favourite grace of Desmond Tutu

A Victorian grace of a child in a hurry!

Accept O Lord this grace,
before we take our place.
Mother scolds, we must not race,
to clear our plate without a trace.

Girl of the Period
Miscellany—April 1869

The No. 1 traditional school grace

For what we are about to receive,
May the Lord make us truly grateful.
Amen

Used by Mrs K. Spring, Headmistress
Loudwater Combined School, Bucks
— and many other institutions

And after the meal

For what we *have* received
May the Lord make us truly grateful.
Amen

The following is a grace composed by a Victorian who believed in the old maxim, 'Little children should be seen and not heard.'
Nora Ellwood aged 90 told us that her father Anthony Ellwood, a Lay Preacher taught it to her and her sister Mrs Mary Raven as little children. She had us in fits of laughter as she recited it obviously indelibly imprinted on her mind—after over 80 years.

Table Rules for Little Folk

In silence I must take my seat,
and give God thanks before I eat,
must for my food in patience wait
till I am asked to hand my plate.
I must not scold, nor whine nor pout,
nor move my chair or plate about.
With knife or fork or napkin ring
I must not play, nor must I sing.
I must not speak a useless word,
for children must be seen not heard.
I must not talk about my food,
nor fret if I don't think it's good.
I must not say 'The bread is old,
the tea is hot, the coffee cold.'
My mouth with food I must not crowd,
nor while I'm eating speak aloud.
Must turn my head to cough or sneeze
and, when I ask, say "If you please."
The table cloth I must not spoil,
nor with my food my fingers soil.
Must keep my seat when I have done,
nor round the table sport or run.
When told to rise, then I must put
my chair away with noiseless foot.
And lift my heart to God above
In praise for all his wondrous love.

Girl of the Period
Miscellany—April 1869

An old favourite

sung by a family with young children
before breakfast on 12th August 1996
staying near Southwold
Thank you for the world so sweet,
Thank you for the food we eat,
Thank you for the birds that sing,
Thank you God for everything.

Edith Rutter Leatham—c 1908
sung by Peter & Elizabeth Dooley & family.
This appears to be the first known example
of a published hymn addressing God as 'you'.

A grace for God to be in
and all around us

God be in our eating and our drinking
God be in our speaking and our thinking
God be in our listening and all we do.

Leslie Stradling
A grace supplied by Desmond Tutu

A Church of England school grace

Bless O Lord the food I take,
and bless me too for Jesu's sake.

Used in Church of England Primary School
collected by Cecily Taylor (1950s)

A school grace

Let us pause a moment
To thank our God above
Who gives to us His children,
These countless gifts of love. Amen

A 19th- century grace for schools

Father, high in heaven,
All by You are fed,
Hear your children praise You,
For their daily bread. Amen.

Children's grace

God Bless the food
that now we take,
to do us good
for Jesus' sake. Amen
A grace used by the mother of John Low

Grace at an evening meal at school just before bedtime.

For food and drink and shelter,
Warm clothes and cosy beds,
We think of those and thank You,
As now we bow our heads. Amen.

The grace for tea

Lord of heaven and earth and sea,
To you all praise and glory be.
I've said my grace: now just for me,
The taste of muffins warm for tea. Amen

Sung Graces

A grace sung to The Skye Boat song.

All gather round for the table is spread,
Welcome the food and the rest;
Wide is our circle, with Christ at the head,
He is the honoured guest.
Learn of His love, grow in His grace,
Pray for the peace He gives,
Here at this meal, here in this place,
Know that His spirit lives.
Once He was known in the breaking of bread,
Shared with a chosen few;
Multitudes gathered and by Him were fed,
So will He feed us too.

Jean Holloway

A grace to share in the kingdom feast

Here is our food and we'll share it on
our journey,
Gathered from south, north, east and
west;
And we'll sing as we eat with Jesus in
our company
Who'll come and share in the kingdom
feast?
We're on a journey, we're on a journey,
We're on a journey, the greatest and
least
And we'll sing as we eat with Jesus in
our company,
Who'll come and share in the kingdom
feast?

Jock Stein
tune: Waltzing Matilda

Thank you Jesus our Saviour

Thank you Lord, thank you Lord,
thank you for all you favour.
Gracious Lord, we accord,
praise to you for ever;
Food from above is a sign of love,
sign of love for ever.
Thank you Lord, Thank you Lord, thank
you Jesus our Saviour

Jock Stein,
tune: Edelweiss

Sung Graces

A lovely short grace from France

Pour ce repas, pour toute joie,
nous te louons, Seigneur.
(For this meal, for all joy, we praise
thee, Lord)
Supplied by Lydia Hurle and sung to
the same tune as:
For health and strength and daily food,
We praise your name O Lord.

Thanks to God, the Lord of time and space.

'Tis God the Lord of time and space,
who plans all things for good;
Therefore to him we offer thanks
for this our daily food.

Jock Stein,—Carberry
tune: "Amazing Grace"

We thank you Lord, for Jesus' sake

We thank you Lord for Jesus Christ,
and for the blood he shed;
We thank you for his risen life,
and for our daily bread.

Jock Stein,—Carberry
tune: Lloyd

Grace sung as a 4 part round

For health and strength and daily food
we praise your name O God
Thank him, thank him, all God's
children, for our food, for our food;
Thank him, thank him, all God's
children, God is good, God is good.
Thank you for every new good morning,
Thank you for all the friends we meet;
Thank you for all that makes us
happy—and for food to eat.
O give us loving, thankful hearts for all
thy goodness, love and care;
And help us always to be glad to give
away and share.

Jock Stein,
tune: "Childhood"

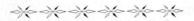

I want to thank you Father, everywhere I go

Thank you Father for all the gifts you
give,
Thank you Father for all I need to live;
Let me share with others, so everyone
will know
I want to thank you Father, everywhere I
go.

Jock Stein, tune: "Ten Green Bottles"

Everyday His providence
increases more and more

God is daily giving plenty from his store,
Every day his providence increases
more and more;
God is daily living in his family,
Nourishing our common sense of new
identity.

Jock Stein,
tune: "Puff the Magic Dragon"

An After Dinner Grace—Bless the Lord

A: {

Bless the Lord O my soul, bless the Lord
O my soul,
And all that is within me bless his holy
name.
Bless the Lord O my soul, bless the Lord
O my soul,
And all that is within me bless his holy
name.

  King of kings—(for ever and ever)
  Lord of Lords—(for ever and ever)
  King of kings—(for ever and ever),
  King of kings and Lord of Lords;
Then repeat <A> once

Compiled by Jock Stein,—Carberry
tune in 'Let's Praise" no 14

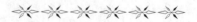

Armed Forces graces,

The Royal Navy grace

Thank God. Amen.

supplied by Michael Mann

Grace on board ship at sea.

"Lord, I've got it down—
let you and I try keeping it down! AMEN"

A W.W. II Naval grace

For food we are about to eat,
For toil of workers in the field;
For the valour of the British fleet
May God's holy name be praised. Amen

H.G. Jones

Admiral Nelson's grace

God Save the (King) Queen,
Bless our dinners
Make us thankful. Amen

A favourite grace and much used by
George Reindorp Chaplain R.N.V.R. 1938—1946

A Royal Air Force Grace,
A grace for the promised feast!

When I arrive on Heaven's landing,
My many sins notwithstanding
And glimpse upon that farther shore
The feast promised by saints of yore.
Then I'll be praising God with all my
might
For the foretaste we'll have enjoyed this
night!

Squadron Leader Leigh Spicer

Army Graces

The soldiers grace in the middle of war

Lord, You have walked with us in the
valley,
You have stood with us on the hill,
You have shown mercy on the dead,
We only ask your pity on the living,
And thank you for providing daily bread.

A grace thanking God for comradeship and
old friends

Thank God for our Regiment and its
comradeship,
Thank God for old friends,
Thank God for food and wine
Through Jesus Christ our Lord. Amen

Michael Mann

A grace for a 'Fathers Night' dinner

Lord, the companies' men, their staff
and their guests,
have gathered to feast in this College
Mess;
But before we all sit and partake to our
fill,
For just one little moment you bid us be
still:
To give thanks for our food and that
with us we have gathered,
Not just our good friends, but tonight
our dear fathers.

Roy McAllen

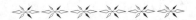

*A grace written for Brigadier Bob
Ackworth*

*He was Chief of Staff at Aldershot H.Q.
when he went to St Paul's as Registrar.*

God bless us all, God bless St Paul's
God bless the Chief of Staff to that place
called,
For food and wine upon this board,
We praise the cook, but thank the Lord.
Amen

Robin G. Laird

*Grace at the Royal Military
Academy—Sandhurst Commissioning
Dinner*

With thankful hearts we praise your
name
and bring you our petitions;
So bless this food and thank you Lord,
for all the new commissions.

Roy McAllen

The Parachute Regiment grace

For good food,
Good friends,
Soft landings
We thank God.

Latin Graces

Benedictus, benedicat,
per Jesum Christum Dominum nostrum."
A favourite Latin grace of Chris Atkinson

*A grace said by the pupil with his Latin
teacher, an old priest, when they shared a
meal together*

Vers: Oculi omnium in te respiciunt,
Domine
Resp: Et tu das escam illorum in tempore
opportuno
Vers. Aperis manum tuam
Resp. Et imples omne animal benedic-
tione.
GLORIA
Priest. Benedic haec tua dona quae de tua
largitate sumus sumpturi,
per Jesum Christum Dominum nostrum.
Amen

Contributed by Charles Taylor
based on Psalm 145 : 14—15

A Latin grace for sharing the heavenly feast

Mensae coelestis participes
faciat nos Rex aeternae gloriae
*May the King of Everlasting Glory
make us sharers at the heavenly table*

Martin Cawley

Graces on Holiday

A grace for a good holiday

For holidays
in this good place
and all God's grace
  we give him praise: Amen

Christopher Idle

A grace for holidays

Thank you, Heavenly Father,
for the privilege of this holiday,
time to relax and enjoy ourselves.
We look forward to making new friends,
sampling exciting food and appreciating
more fully
the wonderful world in which we live.
May we be mindful of others
and do all we can to share our happiness
and may we return refreshed
and ready to serve you in our daily
lives. Amen.

Graces for Freedom, Unity and Friendship

A grace for unity and joy

Father in heaven,
grant that this meal
may unite us all
in joy and gratitude,
and strengthen our bond
of faith and love.
We ask this in the Name of Jesus.

from Margaret Straub

A grace to eat at His table

Blessed be the name of Jesus,
Who ate with drop-outs and sinners
And now he invites us to sit at his table

Leslie Stradling

Grace thanking God for
freedom and friendships

O Lord, in a world where many are
lonely,
we thank you for our friendships.
In a world where many are held captive,
we thank you for our freedom.
In a world where many are hungry,
we thank you for your provision.
Enlarge our affection,
deepen our sympathy
and give us grateful hearts,
in Christ's name. Amen.

Terry Waite

The former Archbishop of Canterbury's Envoy
A prisoner 'in chains' in Beirut for 1763 days.

A reflective grace

As we ask Your blessing on this meal,
And as quickly we reflect,
And as we dwell upon you, Lord,
As so often we neglect.
Now as we are about to eat,
We ask you to accept,
As homage Lord, our thanks,
Our love and deep respect. Amen.

John Allport

*A grace of thanks for peace between heaven
and earth*

Give us this day our daily bread,
O Father in heaven,
who by the blood of your Son,
established peace between heaven and
earth;
and grant that we who gather for this
meal,
may, in simplicity of heart,
taste the joy and peace of Christ.

The Abbey of New Clairvaux collection

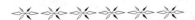

*A grace asking God to transform us
through his love and truth*

God of hunger,
your love feeds our bodies.
Like fire you burn your face
into our hearts.
Transform your truth into human
freedom and courage.

adapted from John B. Giuliani

A grace for unity of mind and heart

Father in heaven, bless our food,
and grant that as we share the same
meal,
we may grow ever more in true unity
of mind and heart.
We ask you this through Christ our Lord

from Margaret Straub

For peace and joy—now and for ever more

We thank you, Father in heaven,
for your bounty from which we have
received.
May your face ever shine upon us,
to give us peace and joy both now and
forever more:
Through Christ our Lord. Amen
  from The Abbey of New Clairvaux collection

A grace for a fragile freedom just achieved

O Lord, for good fellowship in freedom,
and for those who made it possible,
we give you thanks. Amen.

"Freedom is such a fragile thing—
We must treasure it
and continually strive to keep it."
                Gordon Wilson—Enniskillen
Person of the Year Luncheon November 1994
(In August 1994 a 17-month ceasefire by the
                                    IRA began.)

A grace to our shared unity

Lord, bless our shared meal,
a sacrament to our shared unity.
                          from Margaret Straub

A grace seeking world peace

Almighty God,
Look mercifully on us, your servants,
and bless the food we eat in honour of
your name.
Direct the course of this world into the
ways of peace,
so that we may serve you with tranquil
minds and hearts:
through Jesus Christ our Lord. Amen

from Caldey Abbey

*A grace sharing the hope for justice and
peace.*

Faithful God,
Let this table be a sign of tomorrow's
hope already here,
when with the world that hungers for
your justice and peace,
we shall come together singing your
name as our own.

John B. Giuliani

Biblical Graces

Except where shown, this collection of
Biblical Graces, based on the references
given, were written by the Rt Revd
Leslie Stradling, Bishop in the Diocese of
Cape Town, South Africa.

A grace touching on the joy God brings

This day is holy to the Lord;
And joy in the Lord is our strength:
So we'll eat and drink and share,
With great rejoicing. Amen

Nehemiah 8 : 10

A grace to eat and drink
with a cheerful heart

Lord God,
you graciously accept what we do for you,
So we'll eat our food and enjoy it
And drink our wine with a cheerful heart.

Ecclesiastes 9 : 7

A grace for God's care for us all

Lord, we have tasted and seen how good you are
And how those who fear you never lack.

Psalm 34 : 8

A grace thanking God for
all his benefits to us

Praise the Lord O my soul,
and forget not all His benefits.
Alleluia. Amen.

A favourite grace from Psalm 103
frequently used by David Stancliffe

A grace of thanks for God's care of his children—all of us

Thank you, Lord, for the wonders you
do for your children:
You satisfy the thirsty and fill the
hungry with good things.

Psalm 107 : 8

A grace thanking God for his abundance

Lord, we thank you for abundant bless-
ings
And ask for yet one more—
Show us how we can help
Satisfy your poor with bread.

Psalm 132 : 15

A grace for God's mercy

Thank you, Lord,
You give food to all that lives,
Your mercy endures for ever

Psalm 136 : 25

A Hebrew grace

"Hodu l' Adonai ki tov; ki le olam hasdo".
*Give thanks to the Lord for he is good;
for his steadfast love endures for ever."*

from Psalm 136
submitted by Tim Butlin

*A grace thanking God for his
bounteous gifts*

O God, we bless your name for ever and ever,
You give us our food as we need it
With open and bounteous hand

Psalm 145 : 1, 15 & 16

A grace of God's greatness and mercy

Father, we don't deserve even the crumbs under your table,
Yet you feed us with the childrens' bread. Thank you Lord.

Mark 7 : 27

A grace for God's willingness
to share his gifts

Father, your Son was moved with compassion
Because people had nothing to eat:
Thank you for the abundance of your gifts
And for your willingness
To share them with us.

Mark 8 : 2

A grace with God's Kingdom in mind

Father, we thank you for your generosity
In giving us food:
Bring us at last to eat and drink
In your Son's kingdom. Amen

Luke 22 : 30

A grace to God—The Bread of Life

Lord Jesus, You are the Bread of Life
We thank you for nourishing
And sustaining us, body and soul. Amen

John 6 : 35

A grace dedicated to His glory

Grant, Lord, that whether we eat or drink
Or whatever we do,
We may do all for your glory. Amen

1 Corinthians 10 : 31

Everything God creates is good

Lord God, everything you create is good,
And you give us food to be enjoyed with
thanksgiving:
Bless for us this food that we may receive it
gratefully.

1 Timothy 4 : 3-5

Grace based on the feeding of 5000

Here are two versions of a very popular
grace. It is very difficult to do justice to
this grace in translation, especially as
the original was in verse form. It
highlights a grace being brought from
one place to another and then into the
oral tradition. Note the use of the Gospel
story and the emphasis placed on
community.

Father John Baptist Hasbruck from the
Guadalupe Abbey Collection

(i) God, you shared the blessing of the five loaves and two fishes with the five thousand.
May the blessing of the Him who so shared
be upon us and upon our sharing of this food.
Forever and ever. Amen
originated in Rannafast in North-West Donegal.

(ii) The Lord shared the blessing of the five loaves and two fishes with the five thousand.
May the blessing of the God who so shared his gifts be upon our meal and upon our sharing of this food. Lord Jesus, since you redeemed us, bless us, our food and our fellowship. You who live and reign forever and ever. Amen.
from Danta Diadha Uladh

A grace thanking God for the Living Bread

We thank you O Lord, for this food,
but above all for the Living Bread
which comes down from heaven,
through Jesus Christ, your Son, our Lord.
The Ridley Hall, Cambridge, College Grace
contributed by Robin King

Saying Grace with friends

Saying grace when friends visit is a real way of showing our love and friendship towards them and extending our welcome and hospitality.

A grace when friends are present

For all your many gifts of food and drink,
And special joy of loving company,
We bow our heads, and of thy goodness think
And make a glad thanksgiving unto thee. Amen.

A grace for discernment

May He who comes bless our meal
and enable us to discern His coming
in every grace-filled moment of our lives.
from Margaret Straub

At a picnic:

God our Father,
When your Son multiplied loaves and fishes,
He made people sit down on the green grass
Thank you for all this food
And these beautiful surroundings. Amen.

A grace for pleasant music, wine and food

For faithful friends, both old and new,
For each days work and leisure too,
For pleasant music, wine and food
We thank you Lord who gives all good.
Amen.

Robin G. Laird

A Eucharistic grace

At the breaking of bread we give you
thanks
and keep you always in remembrance.

from Methodist Manse roots
collected by Cecily Taylor

For good food and good friends

For good food
and good friends,
thank God.

Joyce Grenfell's favourite.

*A grace for food and friends whilst
remembering others*

In a somewhere hungry,
sometimes lonely world,
for food and friends
we give you thanks, O Lord.

A favourite grace of Malcolm Green

A grace with friends

For fire and friends
and bed and board
we thank our good
and gracious Lord.

Timothy Dudley-Smith

A grace for fellowship in the living Christ

For this food and our fellowship
in the living Christ,
We thank you Lord. Amen

Elizabeth Moore
used at All Hallows Convent,
Ditchingham—Sept. 1996

Thank you for this meal which we share together

Blessed are you Lord God,
Thank you for food and friendship,
And for this meal which we share.
Amen.

James Atwell

A grace of farewell to someone who has been a leader and a friend

We thank thee Lord for lives entwined,
For leadership and friendship kind.
God bless our food and all who dine,
And keep us ever, always thine. Amen.

Robin G. Laird

Blessed be the ties that bind

Give us this day our daily bread, O
Father in heaven,
who commanded your people to come
into your house,
and to eat and drink and rejoice before
you.
Grant that this meal may unite us all in
joy and gratitude,
and strengthen our ties of faith and love:
This we ask through Christ our Lord.
Amen

from The Abbey of New Clairvaux collection

A grace to set one another's heart on fire

Lord, through this food, this gift from
you,
And through sharing this meal together,
May we set one another's hearts on fire,
With you at the blazing heart of the
Universe.

Thomas Crutcher

A grace by those who put their trust in God

Almighty God,
the strength of those who put their trust
in you,
thank you for this food which we eat in
your name,
and keep us always in your mercy and
grace:
through Jesus Christ our Lord. Amen

from Caldey Abbey

A grace for His grace

Feed us O Lord the Living Bread
with the bread for today
and nurture us always in your grace.
For Jesus sake. Amen.

Martin Gilham

A grace for a convivial meal together

Father, as we lift our knife and fork,
May we enjoy each others talk.
May we give thanks with every bite,
And speak with honour in your sight.

adapted from a grace by Peter Morris

A grace for motivation

Lord God, you feed the ravens
And you teach us not to worry about
food:
Motivate us to help those who have
reason to worry.

Leslie Stradling

A grace of thanks and dedication

Lord, we thank you for this food;
bless it to our use,
and us in your service, for Christ's sake.
Amen.

A favourite grace of Barbara M. Burrows

*A grace written on the promotion or
departure of a friend*

For past successes and future ambition,
For faithful friends and tasty nutrition,
For all that makes the soul rejoice,
Now thank we Lord with heart and
voice. Amen

Robin G. Laird

A grace for food and friendship every day

For food and friendship day by day,
We thank you, Heavenly Father. Amen.

A grace to feast with Jesus

Heavenly Father, your Son came eating
and drinking,
Show us how to feast with the feasting
Christ. Amen

Leslie Stradling

*A special grace written by her husband for
a family gathering at Cecily Collett's 90th
birthday held at The Swan, Southwold*

O Lord, we thank you
for the joy and happiness we receive
as members of a united family.
May we continue to count
the daily blessings we all share. Amen

David Collett age 89
June 1996

A grace to God the King

Blessed are you, Lord God, King of the
ages,
You have given us this food to eat
And friends with whom to eat it. Amen.

Leslie Stradling

A beautiful Christian grace
to say with friends

As we assemble round the board,
We do as did our heavenly Lord,
As for his church our Lord Divine
Chose fellowship and bread and wine.

Gerald Priestland

A grace remembering our service to others

Because You call us to be brothers and
sisters
the only fast we celebrate is the bread of
our lives shared with each other, and the
blood of our love poured out in service.

John B. Giuliani

For friends and home

For all the glory of the Way,
For Your protection night and day,
For warmth and food and bed and board,
For friends and home, we thank you,
Lord.

A grace used by Mrs Win Peace

A grace to share with friends

For life and love and all you give,
for all who work to help us live,
for food to share with friends today,
Lord, thank you! Bless us all, we pray.
Amen

Christopher Idle

A grace for everything that goodness sends

For each new morning with its light,
for rest and shelter of the night,
for health and food, for love and friends,
for every thing thy goodness sends:
accept our thanks O Lord. Amen

Ralph Waldo Emerson 1803—1882

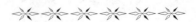

A grace thanking God for all things good

Thank you for the food we eat;
Thank you for the friends we meet;
Thank you for our work and play;
Thank you, God, for a happy day.

*A grace asking God's blessing on our
friends—near and far*

Bless this company gathered here
Bless our friends both far and near.
Bless this table with food now spread
Bless your hand God by which we're fed.
Bless us when our way we take,
Pray keep us safe till at our gate.

Eric Cave

For friends that are visiting

Heavenly father,
we thank you for all our blessings,
we thank you for our friends
and for bringing us together today,
and we thank you for the food
we are about to eat,
In Jesus' name. Amen

Richard Addington

Saying Grace with friends

Football and Cricketers' Graces

*Grace at the 1996 Isle of Man Police
Soccer Annual Dinner following winning
the League and gaining promotion*

For playing soccer with the round
shaped ball
The league and promotion won;
We're grateful, Lord, for your love,
This food, fellowship and fun.

Robin Oake

For Cricketers' remembering Grace!

Where Grace is still an honoured name
we say our Grace for this good game,
digested highlights of the day
at lunch and tea and close of play,
to thank the Lord who makes us able
both at the crease and at the table.

Christopher Idle

A Cricketer's grace

Thanks be to God with heart and soul
that every player gets a bowl,
and sends it down to follow Grace,
with perfect length and healthy pace.
Then we may find, from small beginnings,
some extras, and a second innings;
and with no overs left tonight,
let no leftovers be in sight. Amen

Christopher Idle

*(Cricket is the only game
where meals are written into its rules)*

Some more favourite short graces

A grace for the means to satisfy our appetites

For healthy appetites,
And the means to satisfy them,
We thank You, Lord. Amen

A grace blessing God's holy name

Bless us O Lord, who bless your holy name
and by this food, feed us for your service. Amen.

Celebrating Common Prayer
The Pocket Version printed 1994 p 274

A well used grace in South Africa

Us and this
God bless. Amen

Leslie Stradling

A grace to adopt and adapt

May we O Lord adopt thy creed,
Adapt our ways to serve thy needs,
May we who on thy bounty feed
Improve in thought and word and deed.
Amen.

Collected by Robert Firth.

A grace recognising the needs of the world

Lord, bless our meal,
and as you satisfy the needs of each of
us,
make us mindful of the needs of others.

from Margaret Straub

A grace remembering God's forgiveness

Lord, keep us ever mindful
of your unfailing mercies. Amen.

John Peake

A hymn written and intended as a grace

Now thank we all our God
— Nun danket alle Gott

M. Rinkart.
trans. Catherine Winkworth

Graces Remembering Others.

A grace for a moment's silence
to remember others.

In thanks to God for all his benefits:
Let us have a moments silence
for the hungry of the world.
Remembering others
May we who have plenty,
Remember those who have not,
And may we waste nothing that is good
to eat,
And comes from thy hand O God. Amen.

A grace singing God's praises

We thank you, Lord, and sing your
praises!
You have filled us with all good things.
Hear, then, our thankful prayer,
and open your generous hands to our
brothers,
the starving and poor of the land.
Through Christ our Lord. Amen
  from The Abbey of New Clairvaux collection

A grace for a generous disposition

Let us thank our heavenly Father,
For the gifts of food and wine set before
us,
May we reflect on his bounty and
goodness to us,
By showing a generous disposition
Towards those in lesser circumstances.
Amen.

Collected by Robert Firth.

Remembering people's needs across the world

Grace before a hunger lunch

*or charity meal, bread and cheese, soup n'
pud, Tear Fund, Christian Aid, Oxfam (etc.,)
event.*
Lord, this meal is good and simple;
we who every day have ample
pray our gifts today may bless
those who live on so much less. Amen
Christopher Idle.

Christian Aid grace and offertory prayer
Loving God, take our hands,
Take our lives,
Ordinary as wheat or cornmeal,
daily as bread—
Our stumbling generosity,
Our simple actions,
And find them good enough
to help prepare the feast for
all your people. Amen.

*A grace for God to bring us to
the heavenly banquet*

May the King of eternal glory
Bless this table now
And bring us all hereafter
To the heavenly banquet. Amen.

Leslie Stradling

A grace for food, fellowship and faith

In a world where many are hungry,
We thank you for our food;
In a world where many are lonely,
We thank you for our fellowship;
In a world where many are fearful,
We thank you for our faith. Amen

Donald Coggan

*May the naked feet be shod and
the hungry ones be fed*

Thine are all the gifts O Lord,
Thine the broken bread,
May the naked feet be shod
And the hungry ones be fed.

collected by Haydn Maddock

*A grace for the 'Pop-in lunches' at Holmer
Green Baptist Church*

For food that we eat
and those who prepare it,
For health to enjoy it and
for friends to share it.
We thank you, Lord. Amen.

Doris Croxsan

A grace to make us a blessing to others

Bless us with your gifts Lord,
And make us a blessing to others in need
For the love of Jesus Christ our Lord.
Amen

Mother Sheila

A grace that we may be of use

Lord, bless this food to our use
That we may be of use to you
Through Jesus Christ our Lord

A favourite grace of The Rt Revd
Richard Lewis

The Guides' grace

For food in a world when many walk in
hunger;
For faith in a world when many walk in
fear;
For friends in a world where many
travel alone,
We give you humble thanks O Lord.

> A Favourite grace of Desmond Tutu
> The Girl Guide World Hunger Grace
> also used by the Hunger Task Force
> Anglican Church, Diocese of Huron, Canada.

An adaptation of the same, remembering others in this world

For food in a hungry world
For friendship in a lonely world,
For fellowship in a divided world,
Lord we give you thanks.

> The Girl Guides grace
> adapted by Mary Holliday

A grace remembering to
please others and God

O Lord, who art the first and last,
We thank you for this fine repast,
And ask that we may always do,
What helps others and pleases you.
Amen.

Robin G. Laird

To be graced at our table with the poor

Blessed are you O Lord,
who loves the lowly and the poor!
Grant that we may always find a place
at your table
 with the hungry, the blind, the poor
and the lame.
This we ask through Christ our Lord.
Amen

from The Abbey of New Clairvaux collection

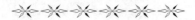

A grace of concern for one another

Heavenly Father,
May our sharing of this meal
Express our concern for one another
And point us beyond ourselves
To the needs of the world. Amen.

Leslie Stradling

A grace for a sensitive heart

For food and health and hope,
We thank you Lord,
Give us also a sensitive heart
And generous hand
To share these gifts with others. Amen

Angela Radmall

A grace to eat and drink to God's glory

The earth is yours, Lord,
And everything in it:
Grant that, as we thankfully share this
meal,
We may eat and drink to your glory.

Leslie Stradling

A family grace

Thank you, Lord, for this good meal
and for the joy of eating it together.

The family grace of Cecily Taylor

Graces for Caring and Sharing.

Family Grace

When we have a meal we begin by joining hands around the table (a reminder of John 13:34) and then together a thanks for our gathering and for the food before us:-

For these and all your mercies, we thank you Lord. Amen

Ivan Mann

A grace to do His work

Thank you, Lord, for this food and,
As you have no hands but ours
To do your work in the world,
Inspire us to find the food
For those who have none. Amen.

Leslie Stradling

Stretch our hearts until everyone is cared for at Your table

Lord, we thank you for gathering us together.
We ask you now to bless us and bless our food
and bless those who make it possible for us to share these gifts.
We pray too for all our sisters and brothers
who have need of friendship and of food.
Stretch all our hearts until everyone is cared for at your table.
We praise and thank through Christ, our Lord. Amen

M. Basil Pennington

A grace using an Acronym
A well thought-out grace by
a very caring person

Send down, O Lord
Plenteous blessings on us and all we
Eat and drink this day;
And may we always
Keep in mind
Everyone who tonight will go to
Rest hungry and thirsty.

Betty Boothroyd
The SPEAKER of the House of Commons

A grace asking God to help us share with those in need

Father, as your gospel teaches,
We must love in word and deed,
Bless us gathered round this table,
Help us share with those in need.
Amen

A grace for fellowship at the table

Bless our meal, Lord.
As we rejoice in the fellowship of the table,
may we also rejoice in eternal fellowship and life with you,
who live and reign for ever

from Margaret Straub

Sharing a meal with friends we love

For food to eat
and friends to love
for heavenly graces from above
we thank you, Lord. Amen

Ivan Mann

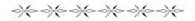

Graces for Caring and Sharing.

A grace thanking Jesus for
our gifts with gladness

To our Saviour let us pray:
Thankful for our every blessing,
Let us praise Him, never ceasing,
Fills us all with food and graces
Thank him for our gifts with praises.

Charles Wesley

A grace for friendly companions and food
on our journey

God, our Creator,
Sustainer and
Redeemer;
give us what we need—
fit bodies
friendly companions
food for our journey, and
faith
to enjoy them, and
to trust you.
In Christ's name. Amen

Michael Saward

*A grace for a place for the pilgrim
to stop and share*

God of pilgrims,
Give us always a table to stop at,
Where we can tell our story and sing
our song.

John B. Giuliani

A grace to ask God's help to love each other

We come to join in the banquet of love
Let it open our hearts and break down
the fears
that keep us from loving each other.

A Dominican Nuns Grace

A grace for total awareness of God's love

Lord, open our eyes to the generosity of
your gifts,
for the joy of human love,
and above all to your presence with us
now.
Then open our hands
to serve those in need.
So, in our sharing of this meal and of
our lives
in your service may we give you thanks
and praise. Amen

Ivan Mann

*A grace to reverence our food
and one another*

Lord Christ, may we so reverence this
food,
one another, and the words shared
between us,
That this meal furthers the healing
and transformation of our lives in You.

Thomas Crutcher

Graces Reflecting on harder times

*A grace from Lancashire during the
depression—1923*

Give us Lord, a bit o' sun,
a bit o' wark and a bit o' fun;
Give us all in t's struggle and splutter,
Us daily bread—an' a bit o' butter.
Amen.

Part of a poem by Alan Clarke
A favourite grace of Norman Turner

A grace to God to make every bit of his
provision count

Mr Jeff Jay, a Lay Elder of Grundisburgh
Parish Church in Suffolk, wrote:
I found this grace in a book, which
dealt with country life in Suffolk
around 1850 when families were large
and food not so plentiful:-

Bless and stretch this food O Lord

Heavenly Father,
Keep us all alive,
There's ten of us for dinner,
and grub for only five.

   from Ask The Man Who Cuts The Hay

Grace for the gift of milk
from a Welsh Black cow

Only those who know what it is to eke
out a living from one cow, some
chickens and a few poor acres, will
understand the feeling behind this
grace for milk the house cow provides;
that was needed to produce the milk,
butter, cheese and cream for the family,
and still leave enough to feed the calf:-

Bless O God my little cow
Bless O God my desire.
Bless thou my partnership,
And the milking of my hands, O God.
Bless O God each teat,
Bless O God each finger;
Bless thou each drop
That goes into my pitcher, O God. Amen.

Celtic Milking song.

*A grace for a place at God's table with all
those he loves*

Blessed are you, Lord,
who love the lowly.
Grant that we may always find
a place at your table
with the hungry, the blind,
the poor and the lame.

from Margaret Straub

From the Selkirk grace

Some have an appetite and no food,
Some have food and no appetite,
We have both,
And may the Lord's name be praised.
Amen.

A favourite of Bernard Morgan

A grace in times without central heating

Here, a little child, I stand,
Heaving up my either hand:
Cold as *paddocks** though they be,
Here I lift them up to thee,
For a benison to fall
On our meat and on our all

Robert Herrick 1591—1674

*Frogs or toads

Favourite Graces for Big Occasions

*A grace asking that we may be blessed
abundantly*

We bless thee Lord, for this our food,
For life and health and every good,
May we more blessed than we deserve,
Live less for self and more to serve.
Amen.

Robert Firth.

A grace for joy and simplicity of heart

Father,
grant that we who gather here
in a community of faith and love,
may take our food with joy
and simplicity of heart.
We ask this in the name of Jesus your
Son.

from Margaret Straub

In fellowship assembled here

In fellowship assembled here,
We thank thee, Lord, for food and cheer,
And through our Saviour, thy dear Son,
We pray 'God bless us, everyone'.

from Marjorie Seymour

A grace for a wedding or large gathering where both children and adults are present

May hosts and guests, both great and
small,
Be truly grateful one and all:
We thank God for this day, this venue,
And all the good things on our menu.
Amen

Christopher Idle

A grace especially for a wedding

Dear Father God,
It is our joy today to share in the
happiness of
(F) . . . . and
(M). . . . .
as they celebrate the beginning of their
married life with us, their family and
friends,
in the simple sharing of this meal
together.
We thank you for the love and labour
which has gone into its preparation,
and ask you to bless this food
for the nourishment of our bodies,
and may our conversation together in
your presence be nourishment to our
souls. Amen.

Bridget Langley

A grace for weddings

We thank you, Father, for all the
wonderful gifts you give.
For food, and those to share it with;
For family and friends, who care for us;
For love and marriage, the strength of
our lives;
And on this special day for (N) and (N)
whom we love. Bless them and us,
Father, with your greatest gift, the
presence of your Son in whose name we
pray. Amen

Christopher Parsons

May the meal that we eat be a treat

May the meal that we eat
be for us a real treat
of fellowship and love
from the good Lord above. Amen

Martin Gilham

*A grace for a factory opening or a
watchmakers convention!*

Eat your bread with joy
and drink with a merry heart,
Because it is now that
God favours your works.

from Margaret Straub

A grace praying to God for short speeches

We pray, Lord, for three things in this
space;
A bowlful of food on every place,
A thankful smile on every face,
And every speech as long as this grace.
We thank you Lord. Amen

Leigh Spicer

Lord, give us thankful hearts

Lord, bless this food to our use,
And ourselves to your service.
Make us ever responsive to the needs of others
And give us thankful hearts. Amen.

> A grace often used by James Atwell

The 'Alka-Selzer' grace

We thank thee, Lord, before we dine
For food and friends and laughter,
So may we feast and drink good wine
And still rejoice—the morning after.
Amen

> A favourite grace of Peter Inge

Grace at a large celebration

Tonight we may reflect as we go off to bed,
No ordinary meal this!
That lies before us on these tables spread,
Dear Lord we thank you for our host,
But, Heavenly Father, we thank you most. Amen.

> John Allport

A Banquet Grace

We meet to eat and drink
good food, fine wine,
But help us first to think
of those less able
with ill health, less wealth,
to join us at our table
Good Lord, aid us the more
to use our talents
for the sick and poor
to better lives for them,
And help us all, both great and small,
To offer trust and love. Amen

Roger Young

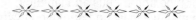

A grace to God for the gifts of food and wine

Before we raise our knife and fork,
or hear the popping of the cork;
Let us give thanks to God Divine,
for his good gifts of food and wine.

said by Peter M. Rutherford
at the R.M.A. Sandhurst
Gaza Company Dinner—July 1996

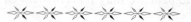

A grace to bless the meal

Father, in the faith of your Son
Who provided food for the multitude
And wine for a wedding,
Bless this table now. Amen

Leslie Stradling

An expandable do-it-yourself grace

This grace has a basic 4-line foundation (or core) but lots more lines can be added if desired. It may suit occasions when several children are at the table, possibly with each one (who is willing!) saying a line — or making up their own lines beforehand. This could work so long as a) it didn't take too long, and b) the whole thing doesn't become more of a joke than a Thank you!

For harvests sown and safely grown,
for daily bread that keeps us fed,
for friends and food and all that's good,
for all your care that we can share—
Thank you, Lord God—Amen

Suggestions for the kind of lines that could be added:
for all the meat we love to eat …
for tasty fish served from the dish …
for fish an' chips an' lickin' lips …
for mushroom, eggs, and chicken legs …
for pie and peas and toasted cheese …
for lamb and ham and home-made jam …
for time to bake a chocolate cake …
for cold or hot inside the pot …
for every slice that's very nice …
for evey bite that tastes all right …
    … and so on!

Christopher Idle

A D.I.Y grace for every occasion

Heavenly Father, we thank you for all
our blessings.
We thank you:
For David and Maureen's 25 years
together
OR
for bringing us together today
OR
for all we have achieved together this
morning
OR
for Barry's birthday
OR
for seasonable rain
OR
for Emily passing her exams
OR
for the end of term
OR
for being on holiday
AND
We thank you for the food we are about
to eat in Jesus' name. Amen

Richard Addington

Annual Celebrations and Festivals

A Birthday grace for grown-ups

Some count the years and some do not;
today, however they add up.
give thanks for all in plate or pot,
in dish and bowl and glass and cup:
God gives the meal, God grant us mirth,
God bless the day of_____'s birth!
Amen.

Christopher Idle

A special grace after meals

We give you thanks, O Lord,
for the blessings received
and for our communion of faith and
love.

from Margaret Straub

A grace for a time of fasting at Lent

May these lenten days be grace filled
leading to the fullest of Easter joy.
In Christ's love. Amen

M. Basil Pennington

A short grace which can be personalised

O Lord, who blessed the loaves
and two small fishes,
Bless (add name or occasion)
and these our dishes.

A favourite grace of
The Very Revd Richard Lewis

Graces for Easter

*Grace for breakfast after a dawn vigil or
early morning gathering*

O Lord, who has woken us up to a new
morning, who has chased the sleep from
our eyes and assembled us here so early
to lift our hands to you;
let us begin by giving thanks to you for
those
who got up even earlier to prepare this
food.
Bless our coming in and our going out
today we pray. Amen

A grace to enable us to share with Jesus

Heavenly Father, your Son at Emmaus
Was recognised in the breaking of bread:
Enable us to recognise him
As he breaks bread for us now.

Leslie Stradling
(Luke 24 : 35)

A short grace for Easter

Hallelujah! The Lord is Risen!
Thanks be to God for his provision.
Amen

Christopher Idle

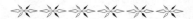

Grace suggested for Easter Sunday Evening

Blessed are you, O Lord,
who on the evening of your resurrection,
opened the eyes of your disciples.
Grant that we who now break bread and
eat together,
may recognise your presence in our
midst:
who lives and reigns for ever and ever.
Amen

from The Abbey of New Clairvaux collection

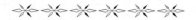

A grace reflecting the wonder
and joy of the resurrection

Father, at Emmaus the presence of your
Son
Made an ordinary meal extraordinary:
Keep us aware of the wonder of his
presence,
At the table and always. Amen

Leslie Stradling

A grace to Him who meets our need

The Lord is Risen—He is risen indeed!
Praise be to Christ who meets our need.
Amen

Christopher Idle.

A grace remembering Christ's love

Merciful Father, your Risen Son,
Prepared breakfast (a meal)
for his disciples on the lake shore,
We ask him to bless our breakfast (this
meal) now.

Leslie Stradling

Graces for Special Dates

January 1st.

Thank you Lord for all things new,
this year, this meal, this prayer to you:
please meet our needs and be our friend
from the beginning to the end. Amen

Christopher Idle.

St Andrew's Day—A grace for Scotland

For Loch and Glen,
For Low and Highland,
For Burn and Ben,
For Coast and Island:
For Kilt and Mac',
For Pipes and Heather,
For Misty Track,
and Bonnie Weather;
And for this food,
Let host and guest,
say, "God is Good,
His Name be Blest!"
By deed and word
all then make haste,
To thank the Lord
And never waste. Amen.

St David's Day—A grace for Wales
March 1st.

For every leek and daffodil,
For rock and river, vale and hill,
For fiery dragons, sport and song,
We raise our voices loud and long;
For all the travels, toils and tales
of Cymru's land, beloved Wales:
Thanks be to God for he has given,
Blessings on earth and bread from Heaven. Amen

St Patrick's Day—A grace for Ireland
March 17th

For Patrick's fame and Erins Isle,
For every Irish song and smile;
For every Paddy and Colleen
And all who love to wear the green;
For all the goodness of this land
For every blessing from God's hand:
We thank the Lord this sacred day,
And truly for our peace we pray. Amen.
© 1998 South Cove Church

A grace on Ss. Philip and James Day

Heavenly Father, the Apostle St Philip
asked
What is the good of five loaves and two
fishes?
As we thank you for this food,
We ask you to have mercy on those
families
Who have not even one loaf today.
Amen

Leslie Stradling

A grace on a day when we have
received communion

We thank you Father,
That you have fed our souls,
In the sanctuary with the Bread of Life,
And now with this food (in the dining
room)
You feed our bodies. Amen

Leslie Stradling

April 1st.

All God gives is for our good;
Let us thank him for our food:
Let us praise him, let us pray,
Let us not be fools today. Amen.

Christopher Idle.

A grace on St Stephen's Day
December 26th

Father, on this feast of St Stephen,
As we ask you to bless our food,
We remember before you,
The hungry children who have no food
today.

Leslie Stradling

December 31st.

Lord, through the year we have been
fed,
with all your gifts of daily bread;
we give you thanks and make our prayer
for all we need this coming year. Amen

Christopher Idle

A farmer's grace

God bless the farmers, bless the farm,
that crops and cattle meet no harm;
God bless our home, our family,
*church, village, friends, community,
Thanks be to God for food to share
and for his daily loving care. Amen.

Christopher Idle.

*or 'our church and this community.'

Graces for Harvest Time

A harvest supper grace

For the farmers who have worked that
we may eat,
For those who have bought and sold
this food,
For those who have prepared it,
And most of all for You who planned it,
We thank You, God. Amen.

Christopher Idle.

A harvest thanksgiving grace

We thank you once again dear Lord,
For all that has just been harvested,
For unfailingly supplying our daily
needs.
May we never take your provision for
granted. Amen

A children's harvest grace

For sun and rain
To swell the grain,
To make the bread
With which we're fed,
We thank you God. Amen

Graces for Christmas

A special Christmas thanks

This Christmas Day,
O God, we pray,
keep us from greed;
help those in need,
and grant that we
may always be
sincere and true
in thanking you
for special food
and all that's good.
This prayer we make
for Jesus' sake. Amen.

Christopher Idle.

A child's grace for Christmastide

We thank you, Lord, for the joys of Chistmastide,
And all this food which you've supplied.
Amen.

December 25th.

Be with us Lord
As in celebration we partake;
And together give you thanks
As we share your birthday cake.
Bring your blessing to us
As we say this grace,
And set your joy forever
on each child's happy shining face.
Happy birthday Lord Jesus. Amen.

John Allport

*A grace at Christmas—thanking God for
his blessings*

For holly's cheerful crimson berry,
For children's faces, shining merry,
For all the people gathered here,
For absent loved ones far and near,
For food to hearten us when eating,
For wine to gladden us when drinking,
For love, for health, for happiness,
For joy and faith and hope and peace,
For countless other gifts beside,
We thank thee Lord, this Christmastide.
Amen.

Robert Firth.

Thanking Jesus on his birthday

Thank you Jesus, that you came,
born for us at Bethlehem,
thank you God, that you have given,
food on earth, with love from heaven.
Amen

Christopher Idle.

*A grace on a freezing winters day
remembering that the wildlife
also need feeding*

As we give thanks for our meal, let us
remember the wildlife, unable to find
natural food in these conditions, and let
us endeavour to remember to feed them.
Amen

Henry Lunney

*The 366th grace for the 29th February
2004!*

On this extra added day,
coming just one year in four,
thank God for the rich array
from his overflowing store. Amen.

Christopher Idle

The Compiler's Remarks on 'Saying Grace'

> The eyes of all look to you, O Lord,
> and you give them their food in due
> season.
> Psalm 145 verse 15

During 1996 for some reason that would not
go away, I felt strongly led to compile a really
good book of graces to include the best of the
old favourites and also to include a good
proportion of contemporary and new ones.

The original inspiration for this book came
from hearing modern and relevant graces,
often touched with a sense of humour, said
each year at large gatherings and celebration
meals, by such gifted people as The Very
Reverend Lawrence Jackson, the Provost
Emeritus of Blackburn, and not only seeing
the pleasure they gave those present, but the
'feel good' factor they leave in our minds
afterwards that reminds us of God's goodness
to us.

A principle aim of this book therefore is to
introduce a large proportion of contemporary
and new graces from those best practised in
the art of grace and verse which could be
found, to take us, in our thanks at table into
the next millennium. Individuals, not only
from the United Kingdom, but throughout the
whole world were approached and invited to
contribute.

Shortly after commencing this venture, The Revd Walter Hargreaves-Wragg B.A., B.D., the former Airport Chaplain of St George's Chapel at London's Heathrow Airport wrote:

"There is a demand for ever newer forms of grace, usually for use BEFORE a meal, and I sympathise with this, of course, but familiar forms can be precious, unless they are uttered with no thought of their meaning (because of their very familiarity). As you know the Anglican Church usually takes the view that a good form of prayer, well thought out and uttered with deep meaning, is often better than an extempore one which tries just to be different. I can see this point, though as a Free Churchman I value the unusual when I hear it, or even use it. So the choice is about equal: well-tried, familiar forms, as against "free" forms which never usually rise to the nobility such as is found within the Book of Common Prayer."

The grace we are talking about as we give thanks at a meal is the free mercy of God, the enjoyment of his favour that cannot be claimed as right, an inspiring and strengthening influence. It is of course a witness of our commitment to Christ and part of the welcome and hospitality to friends.

Whether Jesus said grace before every meal isn't recorded, I like to think he did. But on special occasions he certainly did. All four gospel writers tell the story of the feeding of the five thousand, and how Jesus took the bread and looked up to heaven and gave thanks; and similarly at the Last Supper.

How long people have been saying thank you to God before and after a meal is difficult to say, but certainly for 2000 years. It has become an important tradition in caring homes and households the world over, at gatherings of friends and at major functions.

Saying grace is a short thanksgiving to God before or after a meal, and I have tried to keep to that definition. I was well advised that it is easy when setting out to write a book to stray away from the title, and that a grace should (i) be an explicit Thank You to God and (ii) be short, and it was suggested if I use these as my benchmark I shouldn't go far wrong.

A grace up to 8 lines, I am advised, is acceptable as short. However when I started, I soon found how easy it was to veer away from the best laid plans, and I too have allowed myself a little licence in places.

I soon discovered I am not a purist, having included graces omitting the words thank you; such graces as 'Bless this food to our use, and us to thy service', falls very definitely within this book's interpretation of a grace.

What has been maintained throughout, is that they are graces addressed to God, clearly conveying a Christian message of thanks for the meal, while often including thanks for his many other blessings to us and remembering the needs of others.

I believe God has a sense of humour, and as a number of friends have included graces which they say should go under the heading *Graces for Fun*; I have included such a section. The graces and stories under this heading are to share with the reader that we are all human, and are in addition to the 366 graces.

One of the 'pearls' of this book is 'Table Rules for Little Folk', recited in 1996 by a very dear friend Nora Ellwood aged 90, which tries the meaning of the words 'short thanksgiving' in the extreme, but is a reflection of a wonderful mid-Victorian era when so many excellent graces were written and shouldn't be left out.

It is suggested that when you read these graces you choose the one that strikes you as the most relevant to your needs, as well as hopefully being enjoyable, perhaps adapting or personalising it and making it your own. Then learn it off by heart. Fortunately, not many of the graces are more than 8 lines long.

One way of learning graces is by having them written out on a smallish piece of card and bringing them out in a quiet moment , perhaps during a journey on the bus or train. Two or three graces stacked in your memory bank are really very useful to have, and give pleasure to family and friends.

There are many graces here that are unattributed. Many have never appended their name to a grace, many never wanted to. Other popular graces have been learnt by rote and passed down by word of mouth and many included in this book have come to me in this way, learnt as a child and written down from memory. To those who say grace, many such graces whose authorship is lost in the mists of time are 'old friends'. I haven't added 'traditional' or 'anonymous' beneath them, just for the sake of it, but we can all thank God for them.

One fairly amazing co-incidence was that there were two Richard Lewises who contributed to this book, but not only that; in 1996 they were both in the ecclesiastical hierarchy of the Somerset Diocese. The first, The Very Reverend Richard Lewis, The Dean of Wells Cathedral, and the second, The Right Reverend Richard Lewis, The Bishop of Taunton, hence; unlike others, in order to identify them, their individual contributions are also credited with their titles at the time of writing.

As well as corresponding worldwide for new graces, it has been important to gather graces from a huge cross-section of lay people, because above all we want this book to be ecumenical in its content and outreach. Within two months of starting I had been sent over 300 graces and was given wonderful support by all those to whom I wrote throughout the world.

However; quickly flicking through the pages will reveal the enormous encouragement I received from people like Christopher Idle in London, whose many graces and tireless help so enrich this book. The Right Honourable Betty Boothroyd, Madam Speaker of the House of Commons, The Rt Revd Leslie Stradling—Bishop in the Diocese of Cape Town, South Africa, Benedictine Father John Giuliani of Connecticut, U.S.A., Lt General Sir William Rous who put me in touch with friends who sent over 50 graces between them, and the

Sisters of Mount St Mary's Abbey, Wrentham Massachusetts, who have composed graces, which Sister Margaret Straub has collected together over the years and kindly let me use. She also sent me the addresses of her many friends in the U.S.A. which has resulted in such a good collection of American graces for which I am enormously grateful. To quote a well known Abbey National Building Society advertising jingle, 'Get the Abbey habit', after reciting 18 of the St Mary's Abbey graces, I was getting the 'Abbey habit'!

Saying grace is a habit I would like to see getting re-vitalised both in the home and at all gatherings round the table, and it is hoped by the production of this book you are suitably encouraged.

Acknowledgements

Compiling a book of others gifts is relatively easy, and I have the pleasure of mentioning each one, who has not only contributed graces, but also those who so willingly sent me graces on behalf of others and, who gave me the names of people who added to a collection of graces from which we hope everyone can find one that will meet the occasion.

I particularly wish to thank Emily Hewitt for her invaluable editorial input.

Revd Canon Richard Addington of Charsfield, Suffolk

Miss E.J. Allen-Williams

Revd Chris Atkinson—Brampton Rectory

The Very Revd James Atwell—Provost of St Edmundsbury Cathedral

James Bailey age 7 of Halesworth, Suffolk

Mrs Ann Ball

Mr Nicholas Bevan C.B.—Speaker's Secretary, House of Commons

The Revd Canon Alfred D. Beresford of the Diocese of Cape Town, South Africa

John Bilyard—Lay Elder, of Worlingham

David Bird—Churchwarden, of Saxted

The Rt Hon Miss Betty Boothroyd M.P.—Madam Speaker of the House of Commons

Miss Barbara M. Burrows of Ipswich

Revd Tim Butlin—Vicar of St Peter's, Loudwater, Buckinghamshire

Robert & Sharon Buxton of Tuddenham St Martin

Mrs M. Cambridge of Hopton, Norfolk

The Most Revd George Carey, Archbishop of Canterbury

Revd Canon Eric Cave—Anglican Chaplain—Royal Hobart Hospital—Tasmania, Australia

Father Martinus Cawley O.C.S.O., Guadalupe Abbey, Lafayette, Oregon, U.S.A.

The Cisterian Fathers, Caldey Abbey, Caldey Island, off Tenby, Dyfed

Miss A. H. Chadwick—Ipswich

Private Charlton—The 1996 British Army Boxing Team

Revd Andrew M. Clark—Prison Chaplain

Mrs Ruth Clarke—Southwold, Suffolk

The Most Revd Donald Coggan former Archbishop of Canterbury

Mr David Collett of Southwold

Ken & Sarah Corson—former Methodist Missionaries in South America

Mrs Doris Croxsan—Buckinghamshire

Brother Thomas Crutcher, Nova Nada Monastery, Canada.

The Rt Hon The Lord Edmund Davies

The Rt Revd John Dennis—Bishop of Suffolk

Peter & Elizabeth Dooley & family—Missionaries in Chile

The Rt Revd Timothy Dudley-Smith—former Bishop of Thetford

John Durrant of Great Cornard

Miss Nora Ellwood—Suffolk

The Very Revd Sir Eric Evans KCVO, Hon DD—former Dean of St Paul's Cathedral

Robert Firth of Bury St Edmunds

Richard & Dorothy Fiske—Reydon, Suffolk

Canon Colin Fletcher—Archbishop of Canterbury's Chaplain

Pakinaz Fouad—'Coco' a lady Egyptian Guide from Cairo

Matt Frost—ICHTHUS Christian Fellowship—Soho, London W.1.

The Hon Jill Ganzoni D.L.—Suffolk

The Revd Martin Gillham TSSF, West Wycombe, Buckinghamshire

Father John B. Giuliani—Benedictine Grange—Connecticut, USA.

Malcolm Green MMS—Snr Christian Stewardship Advisor

Father Hillary Greenwood SSM

Joy Grindey—Missionary in Africa

Peter aged 5 and James Halliwell aged 3—of Wrentham

Revd W. Hargreaves-Wragg, former Airport Chaplain, St George's Chapel, Heathrow Airport

Father John Baptist Hasbruck O.C.S.O., Guadalupe Abbey, Lafayette, Oregon, U.S.A.

James Hewitt aged 7 of Loudwater, Buckinghamshire

Paul Holland—Wrentham

Revd Mary Holliday—Methodist Minister

Jean Holloway

Mervyn, Lord Horder—London

Mrs Sheila M. Horsley, Ipswich, Suffolk

Mrs Vi Hughes—Holmer Green, Buckinghamshire

Lydia Hurle, St Albans—a child of God (her description)

Revd Mark Hutchinson Vicar of Walberswick

Christopher Idle—former Rector of North Hartismere

Marcus & Clare Idle—Oxford

Field Marshall Sir Peter Inge GCB—Chief of the Defence Staff

The Very Revd Lawrence Jackson—former Provost of Blackburn

Revd Wilma Jakobsen—Chaplain to Archbishop Desmond Tutu of Cape Town

Mr Jeff Jay—Lay Elder at Grundisburgh

Sister Jill of Hengrave Hall

The Very Revd Keith Jones—Dean of Exeter

The Rt Revd Noel Jones—Bishop of Sodor and Man

The Revd Robin L.C. King of Bures

The Revd Robin G. Laird—Senior Chaplain—Sedbergh School, Cumbria.

Bridget Langley of Kirton Lincolnshire

The Rt Revd Richard Lewis—Bishop of Taunton

The Very Revd Richard Lewis—Dean of Wells Cathedral

Pastor John Lowe OBE—Kirk Michael, Isle of Man

The Revd Canon Henry Lunney—Chaplain to the Suffolk County Scouts

The Revd Roy McAllen—Snr Chaplain Rtd. Wellington Barracks, London

Mr Haydn Maddock, Wargrave, Berkshire.

Mrs Lesley Manchester—P.A. to the Snr Chaplain, Wellington Barracks, London

Revd Ivan Mann—Ipswich

The Rt Revd Sir Michael Mann KCVO of Northleach, Gloucester

The Revd Sandy Millar—Vicar of Holy Trinity Church, Brompton

Revd John Mitson—The Bishop of Suffolk's Legal Secretary

Revd John Mockford—Framlingham

Miss Elizabeth Moore—Lay Training Advisor in Suffolk

Revd Bernard Morgan of Beccles

Revd Canon Peter Morris of Westleton

Revd Canon John Murrell—Walberswick

The Venerable Garth Norman—Archdeacon of Bromley

Robin Oake Q.P.M.—Chief Constable of the Isle of Man

The Revd Roy Overthrow—Bishop's Deacon at Salisbury

The Revd Christopher Parsons—The Riverside Vineyard Christian Fellowship, Teddington

Lucy Partridge age 3—Shrewsbury, Shropshire—1996

Revd Martin Partridge—Vicar of Quainton, Buckinghamshire

Mrs Win Peace, wife of the late Revd Frank Peace—Buckinghamshire

John Peake—Lay Preacher—Snettisham, Norfolk

Father Peter—Guadalupe Abbey, Lafayette, Oregon, U.S.A.

Father M. Basil Pennington O.C.S.O. Trappist Monastery, Lantao Island, China

Canon Simon Pettitt—Diocesan Communications Officer—Suffolk

David Porter—Member of Parliament for Waveney 1987—1997

Angela Radmall of Bury St Edmunds

Revd John Rankin—Stour Valley Group of Parishes

The Rt Revd George Reindorp—former Bishop of Salisbury

Lt. General The Honourable Sir William Rous KCB OBE

Revd Peter M. Rutherford C.F.—British Army Padre—R.M.A. Sandhurst

Stanton Sallows—Churchwarden, Wrentham, Suffolk

Revd Canon Michael Saward—St Paul's Cathedral

Father Paul Mark Schwan, Abbey of New Clairvaux, Vina, California, U.S.A.

Mrs Marjorie Seymour—Southwold

Revd Canon Martin Shaw—St Edmundsbury Cathedral

Mother Sheila—Convent of All Hallows, Ditchingham

The Rt. Revd David Sheppard—Bishop of Liverpool

Revd Canon Ronald Smythe of Reydon, Southwold

The Revd Anna Sorensen—Chaplain of St Felix School, Southwold.

Revd (Sqn Ldr) Leigh Spicer, Chaplain—RAF Honington.

The Rt Revd Dr David Stancliffe—Bishop of Salisbury

The Revd Jock Stein—Carberry, Scotland

The Rt Revd Leslie Stradling—Bishop of the Diocese of Cape Town, South Africa

Sister Margaret Straub OCSO—Massachusetts USA

Cecily Taylor—Poet and hymn writer, Sanderstead, Surrey

Charles Taylor, Director of the Friends of Bury St Edmunds Cathedral

Mrs M.E. Thomson—Secretary to The Speaker of the House of Commons

The Revd Vaughan & Mrs Deanna Tong—Amersham, Buckinghamshire

Noel Tradinnick—Professor of Music, Conductor of the All Soul's Orchestra

Norman Turner of Flixton, Manchester, Lancashire.

The Most Revd Desmond Tutu—Anglican Archbishop of Cape Town, South Africa

Father Chrysogonus Waddell O.C.S.O., Gethsemani Abbey, Trappist, Kentucky, U.S.A.

Terry Waite C.B.E. The Archbishop of Canterbury's Peace Envoy

Revd Terry Wells of Stratford St Mary, Essex

Gordon Wilson—Enniskillen. A man full of forgiveness who died in 1996

Ruth Wilson—Assistant to The Revd J.A.K. 'Sandy' Millar

Roger D. Young of Layham, Suffolk

Reflection on Graces by Christopher Idle, hymn writer and former Rector of North Hartismere.

First Lines Of The Graces

First Lines Of The Graces   *180*